During the Journey

and Other Stories

Sethu

Translated from Malayalam by Aboobacker Kappad

Foreword by K. Satchidanandan

LiFi Publications Pvt. Ltd.
New Delhi

Published by:
LiFi Publications Pvt. Ltd.
211, 2nd Floor, Gagandeep
12, Rajendra Place, New Delhi–110 008, India
Phone : (011) 2574 1000
E-mail : info@lifipublications.com
Web : www.lifipublications.com

ISBN 13: 978-93-82536-64-2 ISBN 10: 93-82536-64-7

First published in 2014

Cataloging in Publication Data—DK
[Courtesy: D.K. Agencies (P) Ltd. <docinfo@dkagencies.com>]

Sētu, 1942–
[Short stories. Selections. English]
During the journey and other stories / Sethu ; translated from Malayalam by Aboobacker Kappad ; foreword by K. Satchidanandan.
p. cm.
Short Stories.
ISBN 9789382536642

1. Sētu, 1942– --Translations into English. I. Abūbakkar Kāppāṭ. II. Title.

DDC 823.92 23

Printed in India by D.K. Fine Art Press (P) Ltd., Delhi–52

Contents

Foreword

Tales of Mystery and Imagination

Sethu, one of the pioneers of modern fiction in Malayalam, is an extraordinary storyteller who conjures up unique existential situations in order to delve deep into the human psyche and come up with rare insights. The stories in the present collection are no exception, happily permitting his narrative magic to survive even an inadequate translation.

During the Journey and Other Stories carries fifteen interesting tales selected from the author's impressive *oeuvre*. All of them prove, once again the principle that short story at its best is closer to poetry than fiction as suggestiveness is the very essence of both the arts as demonstrated by the masters of genre of short story from Edgar Allan Poe, Franz Kafka, Italo Calvino and Luis Borges to Gabriel Garcia Marquez, Haruki Murakami, Patrick Suskind and Alice Monroe.

Look at the opening story, 'A Man from Far-away': A stranger, a certain Mr. Menon, comes to meet Parvathy, a bright student in a convent whose father, supposedly, had died in an accident. Menon claims to be her uncle whom she has never seen. The Mother Superior is at first reluctant to let the girl meet the stranger, but he sweet-talks her into allowing him to have a brief conversation with her. He gives the reluctant girl a birthday gift, asks her about her mother, and her father whom she had seen only in the wedding photograph, tells her he too has a daughter born on the same day and looking exactly like her and she too behaves like a stranger every time he meets her. The Mother's stern voice tells him the time for the visit is over and he leaves reluctantly leaving the girl to wonder who he is and persuading her to look back to see him biding goodbye. The story does not say anything about the identity of the man and leaves us guessing who he might be though there are clues to suggest that he is her father who had probably got estranged from her mother. The beauty of the story lies precisely in this ambiguity.

The second story, 'An April Summer' too deals with a journey: this time of an old man from the village and his niece. The readers like the people they come across are left guessing their destination: the old man tells the auto-rikshaw drivers that he is going to admit her in college and then tells an old woman waiting for the bus that she is being taken to her husband's home. Only at the end it is clear that hey are headed to a hospital. There are only faint hints of the purpose of their visit, in their wanting to meet a particular lady doctor and in an image that rises up in the girl's memory, of her being photographed with a young man in a studio. But the story is important not purely for its suggestive end: the journey too exposes the uncharitable world of lascivious men that any girl going out, even with her uncle, is forced to confront, turning the whole narrative into a subtle critique of Kerala's exploitative patriarchal society.

The title story, again about a journey, this time by train, is typical of Sethu's special genius for creating situations of mystery and awe. Here an old gentleman meets a young man in the compartment of a train where they are alone. They soon begin to talk to each other and the young man says that he knows the old man is a professor—he had had professors for companions in the last two journeys and it was highly probable this time the situation repeats itself. They drink and exchange their stories, the old man telling him of his daughter whom he had lost when she was just twelve. The young man is sure a woman would enter their compartment soon and both are in eager anticipation of the stranger—who the young man clarifies will have some thing eerie about her—when a girl introducing herself as Anita boards the train. Both the professor and the girl have some kind of a déjà vu, a mystical feeling that they have met elsewhere and know each other. This is another story that creates a strange, unearthly and disturbing atmosphere and leaves us guessing who the girl could be and whether she is the professor's daughter who had died very young.

These three stories narrated in a tone that is deeply contemporary, with their necessary suspense, drama and suggestiveness, their profound understanding of existential mystery, their nuanced awareness of the society around us that is growing more and more sick and sombre day by day, and above all the descriptive skill that makes their scenes and characters vividly come alive with a few deft artistic strokes, are enough to demonstrate Sethu's mastery of the art of short fiction. I have no doubt the readers will savour these stories for their doubtless human interest as also for their rare artistic skill.

K.Satchidanandan
Delhi
January 2014

My Journey

I have been scribbling stories for nearly half a century by now, more in mind and less on paper. It has been a long, arduous and exciting journey and on completion of each work, be it a short story, a novella or a novel, I found my life more meaningful, fulfilling and rewarding. I see my stories as endless journeys of my mind through the dark alleys of time and space. In this lonely journey I come across a wide range of human predicaments, at times tormenting, at times intriguing, which take me to unseen situations and unexplored terrains. I do not know from where my characters emerge since many of them have an organic existence and do not tread a path determined by their creator, choosing their own style of narrative, which is not necessarily linear or traditional.

In this era of globalisation and urbanisation, the soft targets have always been the soil (the earth) and woman and my attempt has often been to revisit the unexplored mindscape of desolate, forlorn women. In a highly male-centered society, some of these characters fantasise and stray into the labarynths of solitude, asking uncomfortable questions to those around them and ultimately to themselves about womanhood, man-woman relationship, female sensuality and the overall space available for women in the contemporary Indian society. Amidst isolation and helplessness the thin line of demarcation between the real and unreal planes often becomes thinner for them and they are left to wonder which is real and which is unreal. When the contours of their mindscape dissolve, their solitary journeys often lead them to predicaments where the unreal looks more real to them and vice versa.

I believe that my creative efforts are always incomplete and are completed only in the minds of my readers, in a redeeming and self-fulfilling creative partnership. We are fortunate that we do have a large number of such discerning readers in Malayalam. Some of these stories and novels originally written in Malayalam, have been translated into other Indian languages and English. An attempt has been made here to collect a few of them into a book. I am thankful to Dr. Aboobacker Kappad for the translation and Mr. Binny Kurien from the Editorial team of the National Book Trust for going through the text and offering valuable suggestions. My thanks are also due to Prof. K. Satchidanandan for finding time within his busy schedule to prepare a foreword to the book and also to M/s. LiFi Publications, New Delhi for taking care of its publication.

Sethu
New Delhi
10.01.2014

1

A Man from Far-away

He could perceive an unusual suspicion in the Mother Superior's eyes set behind her thick glasses. She was turning the pages of a thick book carelessly. Meanwhile, she glanced at his face once or twice. Then pointing to a page in the book she said: "No, Parvathy doesn't have such a relative according to our register. When we initially admit the children to the hostel we collect all such details like the next of kin, phone numbers, etc. from their parents. I need hardly tell you that the times are very bad and without the parents' permission we don't allow any visitor, however important a person he is, to see our children. The parents have entrusted their children to our care. You must know that the parents of most children in this hostel live abroad. I mean NRIs. We care the least about their money and pretensions; but we can understand their anxiety regarding their children."

"I know, Mother," he nodded. "I know everything. But this girl, Parvathy is a distant niece of mine. I'm her uncle, whom she has never seen. I, too, am living far-away, and have returned to my native place after many years. Naturally I felt like renewing old relationships. My next homecoming may be after three or four years. Perhaps, I will not come at all. Hence I thought of visiting Parvathy. She was just an infant when I saw her last.... These are things to be given to her."

He put the packet that he had brought with him on the table. The Mother's eyes remained fixed on the packet for some time. Then her face relented a little.

"But, one condition, Mister; will the girl recognise you?"

"How can she, Mother? It is so many years since I left my place. Even my recognising her is doubtful."

A mischievous smile appeared on the Mother's face.

"So I can show you any girl as Parvathy!"

"I don't think a Mother Superior, of all the people, who knows the child's mind well, will do so."

The Mother became pleased a little. Pointing to a chair, she said:

"Please be seated Mr... what's your name?"

"Menon."

"Some kind of identification is essential, Mr. Menon. Otherwise, you can see the girl and give the packet to her in front of me, and then go away."

"That won't do Mother!" he said in a stern voice. "I shouldn't have taken all the pains to come over here just for that. I want to talk to her, alone. That's important. This packet contains some garments and a few small presents. Giving these things to her is rather insignificant."

The mother stared at him in disbelief.

"Do you think that I will abduct this girl? You have a gate and a watchman to prevent such things."

"No, no. Not in the least." The Mother tried to explain with a little embarrassment: "See Mister, it's more than twelve years since I have come here. I have dealt with various kinds of parents and visitors over these years. I'm very particular that these visitors, however great they are, should not trouble the children. At this impressionable age, when their minds are as soft as flowers, they shouldn't have any upsetting experience; I mean an emotional turmoil. I say these things because you seem to be a gentleman. The times are bad. Our society itself is going through a transition. The stresses and strains of daily life are creating unnecessary emotional problems even within the family relationships. Moreover, all values have lost their relevance today. Even love has lost its subtlety and has become something very bitter, vocal and violent. Man's selfishness and greed are behind these changes. In addition to these common trends, we have had some unpleasant experiences as well. Let me tell you about just one of them; the case of a divorced couple. The father was the child's guardian. He was a well placed officer. He had obtained legal rights over the guardianship of the child. Despite this, the child's mother used to visit the girl secretly and would talk to her sometimes in the veranda of her classroom, or in the garden or any other place she found suitable. She tried to influence the child against her father. By the time I came to know of what was happening the girl had become totally disturbed. A lot of poison had been injected into her young mind. Her daddy knew about it somehow and came running to me. He gave me a real earful. You see, he was afraid that being a girl, she would succumb to her mother's tears, and he would lose his daughter one day. I pity these kids. In what way are they concerned about the petty quarrels and misunderstandings between the parents? You know, what happened afterwards? When the mother came next time to see the girl stealthily, I caught her red-handed. That was the first time I was forced to speak rudely to a woman. Then that damned woman shouted at me, 'You, who became a mother without giving birth to a child, won't understand the feelings of a real mother.' You see, I was exasperated. How could she tell me, a venerable old lady in the eyes of others and a mother to thousands of children, that I wouldn't understand a woman's mind! She had really become hysterical; schizophrenic, perhaps. That thirty year old woman made quite a scene in the office room. She howled, tried to pull her hair and banged on the table. Finally she did something extreme. Throwing a wallet containing bundles of bank notes onto the table she snarled 'Take any amount you like, as donation and give me my daughter back....' You see, that was the height of my patience! Gurkha Ram Bahadur had to drag her virtually into her car. She would never forget the humiliation she suffered in the presence of so many children. Hence never again would she have the courage to come this way. Anyway, just think about the impact it would have had on the mind of the poor girl. I have decided thereafter that no such drama will be allowed here. This is an old institution with a good reputation. This is not meant for such cranky people. We want only good children of good parents. The very next day I summoned the girl's daddy and packed her off...."

The man was listening to the Mother's speech with a faint smile.

Finally, having remembered something, she scrutinised his face several times and whispered:

"To tell you the truth, I know this girl Parvathy very well. I can tell you everything regarding her without referring to the register, because she is the smartest girl in her class. We expect that she will get a rank this year and bring honours to the school. In order to facilitate this, I have arranged for a special coaching and some strict time schedule for her. She is a brilliant girl. However, some changes have occurred to her since the beginning of this year! She is always thoughtful and seems lost in dreams. That frightens me. Her age is rather fragile. This is a turning point of her future. If she stumbles now, it will ruin everything.... Her mother comes here frequently. She is an important government officer in some distant town. But she looks quite an ordinary woman. I have told her everything and warned her not to disturb the girl by coming here unnecessarily. She is an intelligent woman. She can understand things...."

While he sat there, the Mother continued, after a pause: "Yes, I remember. Parvathy doesn't have a father. He died while she was an infant. It was an accident. Her mother has a slight limp and two scars on her face. It may be as a result of the accident. I don't know for certain. Her roommate once told me Parvathy has the habit of crying in fear because of some nightmare. Perhaps, she has great attachment for her father, whom she has never seen."

The man straightened himself up and said in a low voice, suppressing his desire to smoke a cigarette: "I am sorry, I'm in a hurry, Mother. I have to catch a flight back. Please call the girl soon, if you don't mind."

Having decided something, the mother rang the bell. By the time the peon came, they had moved onto the outer verandah, fringed by thick and round pillars.

While waiting for the girl, the Mother reminded him once again: "Don't disturb the girl. This study leave is very crucial for her. We expect a top position for her...."

"I know, I know," he nodded.

Presently a tall and slim girl appeared at the end of the verandah. She was wearing a long, loose garment with small flowers printed on it. Her long face was brown in colour. She had big, sparkling eyes.

"Parvathy, this uncle has come to see you. Do you know him?"

With a surprised look the girl shook her head.

The man interrupted suddenly: "She is not likely to know me. Come dear, I'll tell you everything. You may be busy preparing for the exams. Don't worry. I won't take much time."

The girl looked with wide, suspicious eyes at his broad forehead and greying hair.

Wasting no time he took the packet from the table, caught hold of her palm and began to walk.

"Excuse me, Mother! Ten minutes at the most."

They went to the lawn. Meanwhile, she slipped her palm out of his hand; maybe she felt some sort of discomfort in a stranger holding her hand. Thereupon, he put his hand on her shoulder and held her close to him.

"My dear, how long have I longed to see you! Just to see you and nothing more...," he went on raving. Suddenly his throat went dry and he began to cough.

With fear and surprise, the girl turned her head round and took a quick look at his face.

He sat on the lawn near the hedge of trimmed henna plants and made her sit near him. Then he pressed her lean palm gently. Looking into her long eyes greedily, he asked:

"Do you know who I am?"

She shook her head again.

"I... I have so many things to tell you. But the Mother has allotted me very little time. She is much bothered about your study leave and the rank expected of you. By the way, does your mother come to see you frequently?"

"On some weekends," she replied in a subdued voice. "But she won't spend much time with me, because the Mother won't allow it. Moreover, she will have to catch the return train."

"How sad... you have no father!" Once again the girl looked at him with suspicion.

When he found her sparkling eyes searching for something on his face, he felt a little embarrassed.

"So, your mother hasn't married again?"

"No!"

"Do you remember having seen your father?"

"No!"

"Eh? ..."

"Not even his photograph?"

"I've seen the wedding photo, in an old album ..."

"Do you like the father in the photo?"

"I don't know. I don't feel anything in particular. Let me go!" She was about to get up. "The Mother will scold me."

"Sit down," he requested her. And placing his hand on her shoulder, he looked deep into her eyes. She felt something searing through her head causing it to throb. For a second, she sat with her eyes shut and muttered something.

"What did you say?"

"Nothing."

"No, you said something. Why can't you tell me?"

"Mother has advised me to invoke Lord *Guruvayoorappan* whenever I feel worried, and to pray to *Alathur Hanuman* before going to bed at night, to be rid of fear."

He smiled. Moving closer to her he patted her unkempt hair and asked:

"Don't you apply oil to your hair? It is all dry and tangled!"

She lowered her face, without saying anything. He realised that she was in a dilemma, as to continue sitting or run away.

Extending the beautifully wrapped packet to her, he said:

"It's a small present. I know tomorrow is your birthday. I won't be able to come tomorrow. Hence I brought it a day earlier."

When she hesitated to accept it, he placed it in front of her and said in a wavered voice:

"There is nothing much in it. A few dresses for you. I brought them making a guess at your size. But you are taller than what I guessed. Still they will fit you."

Suddenly she said in a stern voice:

"I don't want them, because I don't know you. Mummy will scold me when she comes to know about it."

His face turned pale. After hesitating for a second, he said in a soft voice:

"Just mention my name to her; she knows me.... It's true that I didn't come to see you so far. That's a mistake on my part. But it was not because I didn't have the desire, but I didn't like to disturb you. Anyway now you are a grown up girl. You have become old enough to understand things."

The girl was looking at him intently. She was a bit surprised as well.

"Does your face resemble that of your father in the photograph?"

"Who knows? I haven't examined it."

"Doesn't mummy say anything about it?"

"No."

"Then it may not be so ...." Suddenly he swallowed his words.

Struggling for words, he looked at her face for some time. Then he continued:

"I too have a daughter of your age. She is studying in the same class as that of yours, in a boarding school similar to the one you are now in. I live far away; overseas. I come to see her at intervals of several years. After each meeting we become strangers again. On seeing the look of unfamiliarity in her eyes when I come to meet her, I realise that even my regular letters have failed in renewing our relationship. It's a strange life, isn't it?

"Uncle's daughter...?" she asked, raising her face.

"Yes! She resembles you in many ways. Tall and lean. Wide eyes and a long face. Yes, I can't believe it. If I see both of you together I won't be able to recognise one from the other."

The girl was fumbling with the packet, with an indefinable embarrassment.

Suddenly she lowered her face and said:

"Give this packet to her, Uncle."

"That... she...," he fumbled for words. "I have brought some packets for her too. Her birthday also happens to be tomorrow. A terrific coincidence, isn't it?" He tried to smile.

When she saw the peon coming towards them, she showed eagerness to go away from him.

"Let me go, Uncle; the Mother will scold me."

"Don't worry about it. See, I have so many things to tell you. Hence I require some more time."

"I have a special class now."

"I will get the Mother's permission. She can't be stubborn with me."

"When the peon was sent back, the Mother appeared at the long end of the verandah and looked at them. The girl felt uneasy again and rose to her feet quickly.

"I'm going."

The man held her hand and pressed it gently.

"My dear, I had carefully preserved certain words for you; but couldn't say anything so far. Now let me tell you only one thing, don't hate or forget me, dear." He paused for a moment and continued: "You must be puzzled as to who I am. Okay, I'll tell you; there are several things to tell you. Perhaps, I won't be able to come and see you in the near future. Next year you will get admission in some college. That means you will become a grown up girl. Then you won't be permitted to see me. Hence I would like to tell you everything so that I will be rid of a heavy burden; it has become so unbearable...."

The girl was staring at his face.

"Once my daughter had asked me playfully, 'How can I recognise my daddy whom I see rarely? How is it that only daddy recognises me? Shall we coin a funny password?' Then I told her 'My dear, any child can recognise her father. It was possible even before the discoveries about genes. There is a strong intuition behind this intimacy and recognition. The pulse of life, whose meaning is indiscernible, can also be found behind it. When you grow up and will be able to understand things, the desire to go in search of your father and to find him out will become stronger. You will be willing to go any distance, and even to cross the seas as a part of this search. I am unable to make somebody of your age understand the force that would move you to fulfill that urge."

He paused. It seemed that she did not understand what he said. Her lips were found moving. Probably, she might be invoking Lord Guruvayoorappan.

He continued in a gentle voice:

"Well, you haven't understood what I said. My daughter also fails to understand many of my words. But when I am with her, hold her hands and look into her eyes, she is awakened by a strange realisation. And I can see her eyes widening, nose flushing, and a new warmth flowing through her nerves. That means each and every cell within her is yearning to recognise me. While telling you these things...." He could not continue.

Just then the Mother Superior came near them.

"Enough, Mr. so and so!" Her voice was very stern. "You didn't stop when I sent the peon. Now you must stop it and go away."

"Mother...," he implored, but without knowing what he actually wanted.

"I'm sorry, you have to leave."

"But I haven't taken much time."

"Look, Mister!" The Mother's face flushed. "I don't have the time to argue with you. I took you for a gentleman."

Though he was on the verge of an outburst, he controlled himself and tried hard to smile.

When he turned to walk away, he looked at the girl's face once again and whispered:

"I will come again, daughter."

"Who is this man, girl?" The Mother stared at her with searching eyes.

"I don't know, Mother."

"Then why did you spend this much time with him?"

"He said many things, but I didn't understand anything. But looking at his face, I couldn't be rude with him."

"Girls will have to be a little rude on certain occasions. Otherwise, it will be very difficult to live in this difficult world," the Mother said in a tone of warning. "Anyhow, come with me; it's time for the special class. I won't allow him even to cross the threshold of this institution hereafter. Some fellows have made it a practice to intrude into the institution and disturb the children!"

They were walking. The mother was still angry.

"That too in the month of March especially, when the exams are near and we expect a rank!"

When the girl turned to look at him, without being noticed by the mother, she found him standing near the gate looking towards them.

When he waved his hand slowly she found it hard to turn her face away from him.

Translation of Vaḷare dūreninnorāḷ

✦ ✦ ✦

2

An April Summer

A mid day in the month of *Meenam*. An old man and a girl were hurrying toward the road from the crowded bus stand. The girl was wearing a light red half-sari and a spotted skirt. There was a big saffron ornamental mark on her forehead. She was carrying a shoulder bag. The old man was wearing a short-sleeved shirt, and had a yellow shawl draped around his shoulders. A small bag was tucked under his armpit. An old umbrella hung on his forearm.

The girl was the man's niece. They were coming from a remote countryside. The moment they reached the road, the eyes of the auto-rickshaw drivers who were gathered round a little away, fell on them. Three among them, youthful looking, approached the old man and the girl.

"Uncle, where are you going with this girl?" one of them asked.

"We have come for her college admission," the old man replied in a low voice.

"Is she old enough for that?" the youngster chuckled.

"Is it time for getting admission to colleges?" one of his companions added.

"Anyway, welcome to the town, dear girl," the third youngster said with a mischievous smile while picking his teeth.

"Where do you want to go? We will drop you...."

"No... no, we will walk."

The old man was trying to cross the road navigating his way through the stream of vehicles. Meanwhile one of the auto-rickshaw drivers began to sing a song from a popular film. Some of the drivers beat time with their fingers and others laughed.

The uncle unfolded his umbrella and began to walk fast. The girl found it very difficult to keep pace with him.

The long bus journey had exhausted her. For most part of the journey, she had to stand clutching the long steel rod running across the ceiling of the bus. At last, she got a small part of a seat to curl up. But the old woman who sat next to her turned out to be a nuisance. She dozed and leaned against the girl's shoulder time and again. The girl bore it for some time. Then she was forced to push her away.

It was indeed a tedious journey. Often she would feel nauseous. She then would suppress it by smelling the lemon that she had kept in her hand and distract herself thinking about some other matters. Whenever the bus stopped, she spat out a mouthful of viscous liquid.

The scorching sun had softened the road. Pools of tar were seen here and there.

They walked keeping close to the road. Though the old man had the protection of his umbrella, he wiped his face and neck with his shawl frequently.

Ringing the bell continuously, two cyclists came from behind. Riding too close to the old man and the girl, they went away. Meanwhile one of them turned his head to stare at the girl and whistled lightly.

But the girl did not pay attention to these things. Her uncle's words were rustling in her ears....

She was running up the steps leading to the college, with three or four friends. She was dressed in a light blue sari with leaves and flowers printed on it. There were a few books in her hand. The girl who reached the top of the steps ahead of the rest turned around and called out something, on hearing which the others laughed aloud. There was a mango tree among the buildings scattered above the steps. Some boys and girls had gathered under the tree. Suddenly a tall boy among them, one with a thick moustache and unibrow, clad in a loose coarse Kurta and pants began to sing in a low voice. The rest of the boys clapped to the tune of the song and the girls started dancing. When the song became lively there was more excitement, and more boys and girls joined them. The steps increased in tempo. Heads swayed. Hips twisted. Legs rocked. Colours intermingled. Sounds mixed.... Suddenly a bell rang somewhere and everything became quiet abruptly. The man in the kurta was seen panting. With his body swaying, he looked at the faces around him. Drops of sweat were dripping from his chin. Somebody booed from behind. It was repeated once again. And finally a continuous song....

A bus ran past them hooting the horn loudly. The girl stepped aside with a start. Her uncle was a little ahead of her. He turned around and asked in a harsh tone:

"Are you tired?"

She did not reply. Biting her lips she continued to walk slowly. When she reached near him, he asked again:

"Are you thirsty?"

She nodded.

"Do you feel nauseous?"

She did not say anything.

"Come," he grunted.

He stopped before a paan shop and said to the shopkeeper:

"Give her a glass of sherbet. Add salt instead of sugar."

The shopkeeper was a boy with a green kerchief wound around his head. The girl watched him squeezing the juice of half a lemon into the glass. When she brought the glass of sherbet close to her lips, an unpleasant smell caught her nose causing an up rush of something inside her stomach. She held the glass a little away from her nose. When the uncle noticed her not drinking the sherbet, he got irritated. She flinched at his angry look.

"Drink it," he grunted.

She looked greedily at the earthen pot in the shop yearning to get some cold water contained in it. As her throat was parched, she brought the glass once again to her lips and put it back on the table instantly. Holding the lemon close to her hand she said:

"I don't want it."

"Couldn't you have said that earlier? Simply wasted the money," he growled, flinging the money down onto the counter.

He wiped his face angrily with the shawl. As he was turning to the road, he saw a man standing near him—the black corpulent bald-headed man who had sat just behind them in the bus. He was lighting a cigarette.

"Where are you to?" the man asked.

The uncle and niece started walking without making any reply. Letting out smoke from his mouth, the bald-headed man joined them.

"I think this is your daughter," he said.

"Niece," the uncle corrected him without hiding his displeasure at the latter's intrusion.

"I saw you on the bus. You are coming from a faraway place, aren't you?"

"She has to take a test here tomorrow."

"For what job? In which company?"

When the old man paused for a moment and mentioned the name of a company, the other man looked at the girl and asked:

"Have you prepared well? As it is a reputed company there will be a lot of candidates."

She did not say anything.

"You will get a guide from some shop," he continued.

They walked away without uttering anything. On reaching a junction the uncle halted there, a little relieved.

But the bald-headed man seemed unwilling to leave them.

"Where do you want to go now? To some lodging house and rent a room?"

The old man nodded.

"Be careful; remember that this is a town. Go to a familiar place only."

"I know it," the old man said in an irritated tone.

"I was just cautioning you...."

Without saying anything more the old man pulled away his flip-flop that was stuck in the tar, sniffed noisily and turned left.

"Sreekrishna Lodge in this street is somewhat good," the bald-headed man called out from behind.

Without listening to his words they walked away hurriedly.

A bullock-cart loaded with watermelons was moving slowly in front of them. The watermelon tantalised her. She bit the lemon and wet her lips with its juice. But that only intensified her thirst. Her tongue lay frozen in the mouth like a dead frog. She felt a severe pain in the stomach....

It is a long hall with four or five rows of benches and desks. On each desk there are certain numbers written clumsily with red chalk. Some youngsters are walking up and down on the veranda, with their heads buried in the bulky books held in their hands. Sitting on the parapet, some of them are loudly discussing questions related to different subjects: In which year was the Plassey War fought... Who landed on the Moon first and in which year... Capital of Canada... The place that gets the largest amount of rain... The President of Uganda... Suddenly a bell rang somewhere. Everything became quiet instantly and all of them entered the hall silently, with their heads drooping....

"What shall I do if you walk so slowly? I'm burning in the sun," the old man panted out, standing under a tamarind tree on the side of the road.

He was fanning himself with his shawl. The girl noticed that his face had reddened. She tried to walk fast. But she could not. Her legs were growing weary. She was drenched with sweat. Rain-clouds were gathering in the sky. What a steaming heat!

Her head was throbbing and throat was parched. She tried to wet her lips with the tongue. She wished he had allowed her to stand with him under the umbrella.

"Is it still a long way off?" she asked.

"Your...," through clenched teeth he attempted to say something, but swallowed his words.

On seeing his Adam's apple quivering, her head drooped.

The old man folded his umbrella, and wiped away the sweat once again. A light wind blew. It smelt of cow dung.

"Let's stay here for some time," she implored. But she did not dare to look at his face.

The woman who was standing on the other side of the tamarind tree came near them.

"What a sun!" she exclaimed. The sky has been overcast for the last so many days. It seems, we won't get even a single drop of rain in the month of Meenam this year."

The girl saw her uncle turning his head angrily to the opposite direction.

"How shall we get rain if people go on doing things displeasing to God?" the woman asked as if to herself.

Long milk-bottles were seen protruding out of the cloth bag that the woman had placed on the ground, against the tamarind tree. The girl looked at them greedily and licked her lips.

"It's time for the bus to arrive. I have been waiting for a long time," the woman said.

This girl noticed her uncle looking at her face intently. Somehow, she got a little courage to meet his gaze without flinching. But her head drooped soon.

"We are not waiting for the bus," the old man said, in a weak voice.

A wind blew. The old man covered his face with his shawl.

"Where are you to, then?"

"I'm taking this girl to her husband's house.

"Is it very near?"

"Yes."

On hearing the bus coming with a roar, the woman took her cloth bag in a hurry, causing the milk-bottles rattle.

"How long are we going to stay here? Let's go."

They resumed walking...

She and a young man are standing in front of a curtain with the picture of a garden printed on it. A curly haired man in a coloured shirt is adjusting the camera. As the switches are turned on one by one, the room gets immersed in a flood of light. Hiding under a black cloth, the man in the coloured shirt says, "Stand closer... A little more to the left. Yeah, that's it. Sister's face is to be raised a little more... a little more... Tilt the head slightly. Ready? Smile, please .... No, tilt the head a little more... Ready? Smile once more, please," The camera clicks, and the photographer adds, "Thank you..."

"We have almost reached the place."

The girl could perceive a little softness in his tone this time.

"What are you thinking?"

She did not reply. With a drooping head, she followed him.

"Nothing to fear...," he reassured her.

On reaching the Nursing Home, he stood hesitating on the threshold. Then he turned and glared at her face. She noticed that the softness that she perceived on his face just a little while ago was not there. It was the same stern face she was used to from her childhood onwards.

The old man entered the veranda and asked a man in white uniform:

"Has Thankamma Doctor come?"

"She is there, in room number four. Get a registration card first."

The girl's eyes searched for something. Though the place thronged with people, she discovered a green box in a corner of the verandah. There was a device fitted to its lower part. Keeping the device pressed with his foot, a man was collecting the water that flows out of it in a plastic mug. Another man was seen waiting behind him. Drops of water splashed onto his face.

She could not bear her thirst any longer. Her uncle was standing before the counter to get the card. He did not look round to see what she was doing.

Unable to wait any more she ran towards those drops of water, oblivious of everything else.

Translation of Uccaveyil

✦ ✦ ✦

3

During the Journey

The first class compartment of the train had only two passengers. One of them was a corpulent person of about fifty five. The front of his head was bald up to the crown, and the back was covered with long hair. His beard had turned grey. He was wearing thick glasses. The other was a youngster between thirty and thirty five in bright dress.

He occupied the opposite seat. For a long time they sat without mutual introduction. The bearded man had a fat book in his hand and many magazines beside him. He did not raise his eyes from the book for long. The youngster, may be weary of sitting silently, snapped his fingers time and again and muttered something to himself. After a while, he took a piece of chewing gum from his pocket and began to chew it staring at the dry soil that was running backwards.

At times he gazed at the bearded man, but the latter was not aware of it. The apples of his eyes were moving along the lines of the book.

A little later the young man coughed aloud. Still the bearded man did not respond. However, when the former began to hum a song sung by Noorjahan, the latter sat upright, kept the book aside, took off his spectacles, rubbed it, turned his head to the outdoor scenes and brought his eyes back to the book again.

Will this situation continue throughout the one-and-a-half-day-long journey? The young man felt weary. At last, having decided to intrude upon the other, he leaned forward with a smile and said:

"Hello Professor, I'm Sudheer—Sudheer Sreevastav."

The bearded man was surprised. He put his book aside, twisted his face a little and gazed at the other man curiously. Then he spoke in a sonorous voice:

"Hello. But how did you know that I'm a professor?"

"Oh!" Sudheer laughed. "That's my hobby. While travelling in a train, walking through the streets, sitting at the beach and parks, if I have nothing to do, I observe those nearby with a view to guessing where they belong to, which language they speak, what is their occupation and so on. You can find out all such details from their features and behaviour if you try earnestly. And my observations hardly go wrong."

"Wow! Smart boy!" The professor's voice reverberated in the compartment. "Can you guess what my subject is?"

"History." Sudheer was sure of his answer.

The Professor's eyes widened in surprise.

"Correct. But how could you...? Is it from my thick spectacles and sharp piercing eyes that bulge out of it or from my baldness? Have I got the slimy look of a historian?"

"Sorry Professor." Sudheer laughed. "I don't wish to disclose my professional secrets."

"No friend, you needn't. Now let me guess about your profession."

"Welcome."

"Company Executive? Multinational, perhaps?"

Sudheer shook his head in the negative.

"Marketing?"

"No."

"Financier?"

"No."

"Then?"

"Personnel, of all things." Sudheer burst into laughter. "A line which you could not have guessed. It is through that job I developed my ability to study men closely and assess their personality."

"Wow! It's a fine thing to have interest and patience in observing and trying to understand others. That is also a type of personnel management."

"But sir, now-a-days our work does not need much mental faculty. With some tricks, a little tact and enough guts we can manage it somehow."

Then he began to tap his thigh gently, pondering over something.

"Even in management there is a rhythm, isn't it Sudheer?"

Sudheer did not seem to have heard it. He continued to tap his thigh in accordance with some tune passing through his mind.

"Anyway the ice has been broken," he said after a while. "Till now I was so bored. I haven't kept mum so long since my childhood. That's my nature. My mother used to say that I'm unable to sit without chattering even for ten minutes. If there is nobody to listen to me I will speak to myself. That is the last resort. First, in my mind. Then it starts coming out. Presently I will imagine that somebody is sitting before me as a listener, and will go on talking ceaselessly."

The Professor seemed much amused. Lighting a cigarette, he said:

"Sudheer, perhaps PR will be the subject suited for you."

"Sir, this PR is not something you can find in any book or taught in any institution. However, I am not that good at Public Relations."

"I have seen many extroverts like you retiring into their own shells after a stage."

"Maybe. That is also a possibility. Perhaps when I reach your age, I may also change like you and become mature."

"Nothing of the kind, Sudheer. It has nothing to do with age. This is only an interesting peculiarity of one's personality. I do like such persons. They have a great quality that I don't have."

"I think professors are generally very communicative."

"It may not be so. I myself am a very good example. I can spend a whole day without talking to anyone. I do prefer to speak to myself. I have matters within me to tell, discuss, quarrel and compromise with myself. It is quite difficult for me to convince myself before doing anything. But in the presence of somebody I simply stammer. And my inability to communicate effectively with others, aches me a great deal."

"I have heard that is possible through practice."

"That is not true in my case. I've tried a lot, but failed miserably. Perhaps it is an inborn ability."

"Anyway, it is good you got into my compartment. It is extremely boring to travel along this dry and parched soil for one and a half days without a company."

The Professor smiled. He took a paper packet from his bag and asked:

"Do you like pakora. It may be a bit pungent. It has been cooked by my wife."

"Doesn't matter. I too am an admirer of the pungent taste of chilli."

"I always keep many pakoras and water with me on long journeys to avoid boredom," the Professor said with a laugh.

"There is a reason behind my discovery that you are a professor. You may find it hard to believe. A curious coincidence."

"Speak out; I am ready to believe any strange bit of information."

"This is my third journey along this route, and I always got this very compartment. And strangely enough, in the beginning of the journey there would be just two passengers—one professor and I."

"Hah! Hah! Hah! It seems that you cannot travel through this route without coming across a professor. In a sense that's true. The population of professors in our country is increasing day by day. And they are crazy about travelling."

The professor's laugh echoed within the compartment. It reverberated for a long time without dissolving in the rhythmic sound of the train.

"I think you won't say that History itself was the subject of the professors of your previous journeys too."

"No sir, one of them dealt with Philosophy and the other, hold your breath, Parapsychology."

"An assorted group, isn't it? Candies in a chocolate box."

"That turned out to be good, anyhow. I could hear them talking about many topics. And there was nothing handy to me, except a few oft-repeated jokes and bluffing. But they had plenty to share compassionately with a stupid fellow like me. How vast their world is! I envy them. Take the example of the Parapsychology professor. He was doing research on rebirth."

"Professor Mitra—Chandan Mitra?"

"Of course. Do you know him?"

"We have studied together at Kashi for a long time. But it is long since we met."

"That was an interesting journey. Now I feel a strong urge to travel again and again through this route. I am yet to meet professors well-versed in Science."

"But this time it will be quite boring, comrade. I am unable to speak so amazingly as Professor Chandan."

"It's all right." Sudheer laughed. "No company is boring to me. You people just speak on matters that you know about, right? I do like it. But we are not like that. We speak about anything under the sun, authoritatively. A kind of occupational hazard, of course."

"Chandan might have told many interesting stories, didn't he?"

"Of course. He had many things to tell. Like a dull child I kept on listening to him with my mouth wide open. The day passed without my being aware of it. In fact, before our departure I had become a great admirer of him. And we wrote to each other for a short period. He had asked me to inform him of any curious matter or incident that came to my notice. Later on our correspondence came to an end somehow. Nor could we meet afterwards."

"Chandan is exceptionally intelligent."

"That meeting has prompted me to believe anything. I think everything is a possibility. If somebody comes and tells me that he saw you flying on wings over the fort of Old Delhi, I will believe it. That's a great possibility. A historian can surely fly on wings over that old debris. He should be able to do that. How can a man who cannot grow his own wings be called a researcher?"

Caressing his beard and pondering over something, the professor kept mum for a while and then said:

"That's right, Sudheer. It seems to me that our life is the sum of several fables that are difficult to believe. Not only history, man's journey through past, present and future, too, seem to be a fable. An attempt to analyse everything in the light of science is quite boring. Without these myths life will be quite dry. I hate the botanist who dissects a beautiful flower presented by the benevolent Nature."

"I can find out at least five possibilities if an ordinary man behaves strangely in a particular situation. I am even ready to think at length about those possibilities without the support of any scientific theory and also to believe to a great extent in the possibilities that emerge out of the thinking."

"That is right Sudheer. We all look forward to our tomorrows clinging to several possibilities. Even while separating the strands of yesterday quite strenuously, we keep open the windows of many such possibilities, knowingly or unknowingly."

"Leave it, sir. Let's think about this very compartment. A compartment with four well defined boundaries. Do you think that we two will be the only passengers in this compartment throughout this one and a half days' journey?"

"No, nothing of the sort," the professor shrugged his shoulders. "Anyone can enter this compartment. Perhaps two more passengers may enter from any station on the way before it gets dark and they may leave the compartment next morning. Then some others in their place."

"But sir, that is not going to happen," Sudheer asserted. "Only one person will step in. And that too a beautiful lady!"

"How can you be so sure?"

"That is a great possibility. That was what happened during my previous journeys."

"Why can't it be different this time?"

"I'm sure it won't be different."

"Intuition?"

"I am not at all interested in that cliché."

"Then?"

"That's a strong possibility."

"Hah! Hah! Hah!" The professor laughed. "How can you be sure of it?"

"Professor, it is impossible to find a reason for these things. We can only say that it happens so."

"Friend, isn't it a kind of evasion? There should be a specific reason for everything."

"Not necessarily. It is this insistence on having a reason that creates problems. A number of incidents, whose reason or significance is unknown to us, take place around us. If we try to find out the reason, we will end up in sheer darkness."

"By the way, from where will she get into? Who is she?"

"I don't know. She may turn up from anywhere before getting dark."

"Alone?"

"Yes."

"Who is she?"

"Sir, I just don't know."

Sudheer sat silent for a long time looking outside. The sun had begun to descend behind the distant Palmyra woods. The professor saw his face blushing while looking at the dry soil. A warm breeze was rushing in. Tying his handkerchief on his head, Sudheer started humming a Hindustani tune, along with a rhythmic tapping on his thigh. After a while he stood up and looked at the professor, a little perplexed.

"Sir, why should we waste this fine evening? If you don't misunderstand my openness, let me offer you a drink."

The professor smiled. "Though my friends have observed that I have the look of a drunkard, I'm least interested in such things. I have tasted it, of course. When I happen to be in a pleasant company, I will have a drink only if they compel me. That's all. One should be able to drink with the maximum enjoyment. There lies the thrill."

"If you find my company not bad...."

The professor nodded.

Sudheer took a bottle and two plastic glasses from his bag. Pouring whiskey into the glasses he said:

"Hope you have water with you. I just don't want water."

He raised the glass. "For the unknown guest whom we are awaiting."

When the professor was about to bring his glass close to his lips, he saw Sudheer emptying his glass in one gulp. Then he shook his head, drank a mouthful of water making unnecessary sounds and ate two pakoras.

"Usually I drink when it grows further dark. Our guest may be here at any moment and that's why I made it a little earlier today. Isn't it indecent to drink in the presence of a woman who is a stranger?"

"Oh! I didn't think about it."

"If you don't mind let me have two more. That is my quota. I know this is excessive, but I have become used to it. While at home, I will manage it in single large gulps inside the bathroom or beneath the staircase, evading the eyes of my Father and Uncle."

"All right," the professor nodded. "For me one glass is enough. I will go on sipping it little by little."

While the professor was watching him curiously, he went on chewing pakora and gulped two more glasses of whisky. Then he closed the bottle, tucked it into his pocket and lit a cigarette.

"My wife might not have thought that her pakora would have such an unholy experience."

"I beg her pardon. By the way I forgot to ask. Your family?"

"Family means only my wife and I."

"Children?"

"I had a daughter, but she is no more."

"Oh! I'm sorry."

"She passed away in her childhood, when she was twelve."

He closed his eyes for a while. Then he gulped what was left in his glass. While handing over the glass to Sudheer he muttered:

"It was just pneumonia—a disease that can be cured by any physician."

Sudheer found the professor's face growing gloomy. He stood up and switched on the light. It was beginning to get dark outside. Shadows of the palmyra trees against the western horizon had begun to fade. The distant barren hills began to be covered with mist.

"What about your family, Sudheer?"

"Father, mother and a younger sister."

"Aren't you married?"

"I haven't thought of it so far. I will have to when I find it inevitable. A marriage should be a fine companionship. Or else it will be highly boring."

"By then you will be quite old."

"Never mind, sir," Sudheer said with a laugh. "All of us are waiting for some curious possibilities."

The professor kept silent.

Time was passing by. The outside scenery was dipped in thick darkness. The train seemed to dive through a huge cave of darkness. Along with the changing rhythm, Sudheer began to hum a tune.

"Sudheer, she hasn't come yet," the Professor reminded him.

"She will, sir; definitely. That's such a great possibility."

"Perhaps from the next station."

"Maybe."

"Who is she?"

"I'm quite ignorant of that, sir. She may be anyone. On the first occasion it was an artist. A young maiden going to a festival to perform some dance. She had a dance-like rhythm both in her movements and eyes. The next time it was a newly wedded bride going to her husband's workplace. A bashful woman, who had covered her head with her sari and had vermillion on top of the forehead. A typical Indian woman."

"Well, who can it be this time?"

"I can't make any guess sir. It can be anyone."

By then the train had reached the next station. After the long journey through darkness, when they came to the station flooded with light and all kinds of sounds, they looked out of the compartment eagerly. Passengers were running hither and thither with their knapsacks and bags. The professor and his companion scrutinised the running crowd with the hope of finding a girl looking for the first class compartment. Walking towards the compartment door and opening it, Sudheer sent his searching eyes to the platform. People were rushing into other compartments. The platform witnessed the crowd of a festival.

Stretching his head further, Sudheer looked at the platform again. Is there a slim tall girl of medium complexion among the crowd?

At last the bell rang and the train started moving to a short whistle. Sudheer returned to his compartment with bent head.

"She hasn't come, Sudheer." Sudheer noticed the disappointment in the professor's tone.

"Do you believe that she won't come?"

"Now I am tempted to believe so."

"Let me ask you something if you won't misunderstand me. I don't know whether it is proper on my part to ask this kind of a question to a person of your calibre and age."

"Never mind, speak out. Aren't you my young friend?"

"Of course, but how can I—?" Sudheer hesitated further and then came out with the question: "Do you sincerely wish for her to arrive?"

The professor was embarrassed. He tried hard to hide his blushes in a smile. Then he put a cigarette between his lips and opened the match box. On finding it empty, he became angry and threw it outside. Sudheer noticed the tension on the professor's face while he was lighting the cigarette with a lighter.

"It's true Sudheer," he said in a low voice. "Why should I lie to you? Since you talked about that possibility, I have been thinking only about her. I don't feel ashamed of confessing it. I desire for her arrival. I long to see her. I'm ready to wait for her. Perhaps until too late in the night, when the last passenger gets into the train. Let's not bolt the door. A knock may be heard at the door any time. Yes, far from being just a possibility, it has become a certainty now."

Finishing his words somehow, the professor began to breathe hard with fatigue.

"Professor, I hope you are all right. May I offer you a small drink?"

"No."

"Have a small, sir"—Sudheer insisted.

"No Sudheer, it will make me ponder over unnecessary things."

The train began to speed up.

"She may turn up at the next station, perhaps. We will reach there within half an hour. If she is not seen there, we needn't wait for her. Nobody may turn up after nine o'clock."

"Sudheer, you are shutting the window of a great possibility very cruelly. Though we were simply glorifying that possibility, now it seems a reality."

"At times it happens so, sir. Sometimes we get confused to distinguish between truth and illusion. Anyway, I'm not ready to reject that great possibility."

"I do believe you, my young friend. May be because there is no other option before me."

The professor stood up and began to pace up and down.

"My daughter Arati passed away when she was twelve. Though she was of a dark complexion, her face was beautiful. She had long dark eyes. When she smiled her eyes would expand, and that would illuminate our house. She used to sing and draw pictures. Within the short span of twelve years she gave us sweet memories of our last thirty years and closed her eyes forever."

The professor's voice faltered. Sudheer saw his fingers shivering when he wiped his eyes with his handkerchief.

"She was my dearest companion. In fact I was always a crazy child who longed to collect the meteors that fell down unexpectedly, and to store them in a glass jar. We had a small world of our own. She was gifted with many accomplishments that I longed to have in me. Her large eyes imprisoned me. She was the beginning and the end of all for me. After her death I have become a mere shell."

"Sir," Sudheer said softly, "now I see you flying over the forts of Old Delhi."

"Sudheer, you are trying to change the subject."

"Sir, that's the primary tactics of personnel management. We are clever at chess. It is through clever moves and, if inevitable, through foul play, that we move forward always. Those moves will lead us to gains as well as losses and at times even to relinquishment. To win some way or the other is our sole concern."

"You people will have only certain situations to handle, Sudheer. For that some tricks and tactics will do. Whether it is politics or management the tactics adopted are more or less the same. But in the case of family ties, there are several situations leading to unexpected defeats that cannot be tackled by mere tactics. Sometimes we may be slapped even before we start thinking."

"I do know about such things, sir,' Sudheer interrupted. "However, I thought it would be fine to change the subject. That's all."

The professor returned to his seat and sat on it in a leaning posture, closing his eyes. Sudheer saw his lips trembling. Is he reconciling himself to something or praying? Sudheer kept waiting. He thought it improper to disturb the Professor in that state. Still he was impelled to continue:

"Have you ever spent a whole dusk alone among those ancient forts and historical remnants? I've experienced it several times. Once, during a summer dusk, I ate bhang for the first time and lay there on my back. After a while the forts around me seemed to grow high and touch the sky, and I felt as if I were a solitary prisoner lying in one of the dark rooms of that huge prison. Beyond the colossal outer walls I could hear the sound of horse-hoofs. Emperors who lost their crowns and princes who slew their siblings for throne came out of the pages of history. The swords in their hands were dripping blood. Royal chambers with never ending musical concerts.... Painted feet moving in tune with the music.... Rhythmic tinkling of anklets.... I was walking backward through time. Then I became a prince who lost his crown, and a fakir wandering around the world with some holy books, in search of an honest man. Bells tolled around me. Devotional songs were flowing into my ears from all sides. Then I woke up, sat cross-legged and started to sing a devotional song that I learned in my childhood. What prompted me to pray even though I was sure that nothing was going to happen to me? Was it to escape from the imprisonment of bygone generations, and from the duties of history? Or to get a firm footing in the present that has well-defined boundaries?"

It was when the professor shook him by the shoulder Sudheer realised that he was babbling something with his eyes half-closed.

"Sudheer," the professor said patting on his shoulder: "As far as I am concerned, History is a great support. Without that support there is no present and future. When we try to find out the relevance of our thoughtless deeds, and even the irrationality of this endless waiting, we reach the various transitional periods in History."

"I don't understand, sir."

"Never mind, Sudheer." The professor patted on his shoulder again and added: "I've taken just a single drink."

The professor's laugh echoed in the compartment. The train began to slow down as it was approaching the next station. "Sir, I think we are about to reach yet another station."

"Yea."

"Before that, if you don't misunderstand me, let me ask you something. Don't think I am misusing the my liberty with you. How will you regard the girl who is about to enter the compartment?"

The professor's look fixed on his face for some time.

"What do you mean?"

"I mean.... Don't we desire to have, at least in our mind, some unknown relation with those whom we meet and those who fascinate us? A little curious relation?"

"Oh, that? I am quite ignorant of it, my friend. Woman is one and the same in my eyes—a life force with many faces. Various manifestations of the same force. If you look from a different angle, all these faces and relations will appear one and the same. These various relations will attain the same nature as a complementary force in man's journey from incompleteness to completeness."

"Somehow, it seems to me that the girl who is going to get into our compartment is related to one of us in some way."

"How can you say that?" the professor asked with the same look of wonder.

"Or else we won't be waiting for her arrival so excitedly. So that's a great possibility."

"Your theories of possibility are beyond my limited intellect. I feel far inferior to you all of a sudden. Usually I do not allow anyone to belittle me."

The professor laughed aloud. The same reverberating laugh. Refusing to dissolve in the rhythmic sound of the train, that rippled in the compartment.

Some light appeared at a distance. The speed of the train decreased. Sudheer sprang up from his seat. Placing his hands on the bars of the window, he looked out.

They did not have to wait long. A tall slim girl stepped into the compartment with a shoulder bag and a box. Placing the box below the seat and getting seated comfortably, she looked at them with a smile.

"I'm Anita," she introduced herself.

Sudheer was looking at her in astonishment. A slim girl of medium complexion in a loose Kurta and Churidar. Her face had a youthful shine. Her large eyes seemed to fill her entire face. When she smiled, her eyes widened and the compartment seemed to get illuminated further.

When Sudheer glanced at the professor, he saw him sitting stunned. He was scrutinising the girl as if seeing something unbelievable. While putting his spectacles back on his face after wiping it several times, his lips murmured: "Never; it won't be. It won't ever come true."

"Am I causing you inconvenience?" The girl asked in an extremely cold voice. There appeared a strange glitter on her face.

The professor was still in the same posture, breathless and dumbfounded. Tension was mounting on his face. His Adam's apple was seen rising up.

"Sir," Sudheer called in a low voice, "let's have our meals. Should I fetch something?"

The Professor did not seem to have heard it. His eyes were still on the girl's face. And his dried lips were still murmuring.

Unable to comprehend the meaning of his look, Anita turned her face away. But she was heard saying:

"Sir, I have seen you elsewhere, but can't remember where it was."

"He might have taught you," Sudheer interrupted.

"Hey, No!" Anita said, still trying to recollect their previous meeting. Her eyes widened abruptly. "Somewhere else, some special place. A very intimate meeting. But I can't remember where it was."

The professor stirred a little. He sat upright and looked at Sudheer woefully and asked in a hoarse voice:

"Do you remember Chandan's address?"

"It may be found in my diary."

"I want it."

"Why not, I will give it to you."

Sudheer slowly stepped onto the platform, lighting a cigarette. The platform was deserted. The red signal light was seen far away. Sudheer realised that the train would be kept there for some time. He felt hungry and thought of eating something. The professor also must be hungry, he thought. Moving closer to the window he peeped into the compartment. But the professor did not notice him. His countenance seemed to have changed totally. Getting rid of his initial bewilderment, he has moved closer to Anita. He was saying something to her continuously. The expressions seen on his face seemed inscrutable. Those changing expressions resembled very thin pieces of some filmy substance floating through the air from somewhere, and getting stuck to and falling off his face by turns. Anita was listening to him intently with the curiosity of a girl listening to some tale from her grandmother.

Filled with amazement, Sudheer kept on watching them. The girl's eyes resembled two little stars below her curved eyebrows. They twinkled within their sockets. Within no time they seemed to widen and fill her face as a whole. Presently it appeared that there was nothing but eyes on her face. All of a sudden, the compartment seemed to have plunged into darkness and the professor was seen shrinking into a corner unable to bear the blazing light coming out of her eyes. Sweat was streaming down his forehead and cheeks.

"Professor...," Sudheer called him, tapping on the bars of the window. "Are you all right?"

The reply was only a groan. His languid body shivered a little. The chest was rising and falling. The bewildered Anita was seen moving closer to him.

Sudheer rushed into the compartment and found the Professor curled up and breathing heavily. When Sudheer began to rub his chest, the professor gesticulated that he was all right. He sat straight strenuously with a distorted smile. After a while he began to whisper in broken words:

"Beyond the light years, from the milky way comes this guest. Such unexpected guests will have some strange extraterrestrial messages to be conveyed to us. Please allow me to receive this guest, who has come after a long gap of Ages. I'm still a child who yearns to preserve in glass jars the meteors that fall down unexpectedly."

Sudheer kept silent. He simply nodded his head. Then, he opened his bag and began to search for Professor Chandan's address.

Translation of Yātrakkiṭayil

✦ ✦ ✦

4

Yet Another Summer

She opened the door and looked out again. The young man was still there in the corner of the veranda, sitting curled up. He was lean and bent. His hair was a mass of tangles and beard was thin. His shirt and dhoti were dirty. It seemed he hadn't taken a bath for days or changed his clothes. The stench of his sweat reached her nose even though she was standing away from him. He scratched between his hairs frequently with fingers that resembled dry twigs.

"Haven't you left yet?" she asked him, stepping onto the veranda with a kerosene lamp in her hand.

He did not say anything; nor did he turn round. He killed a louse that was stuck between his fingers and stared into the darkness.

"What's your name? Where do you come from? Have you run away from home?"

She did not get any reply to these questions too.

The darkness that was melting in the heat of Meenam seemed to have percolated and coagulated to form thick lumps here and there. The man breathed with a disgusting groan, and coughed persistently. The sounds that escaped his throat lost their rhythm because of the phlegm.

"Anyway, if anybody happens to see you sitting here, that'll put me to disgrace. My kids' father will come home on leave next month," she said, shaking her head and staring into the darkness.

Once again he showed no sign of having heard her. With a jerk of his head he took a beedi from the folds of his dhoti at the waist and placed it between his lips. His fingers shivered when he was striking the match. In the light of the match that lasted just a second she could see a long scar on his cheek.

Somebody passed along the alley just beyond the fence, flashing a *choottu** in his hand.

"If you don't have the money to pay the bus fare, take it from me and go away. The last bus to the town leaves around 9.30. Be careful not to put the butt of the beedi in the courtyard. Somebody may see it at dawn."

Without listening to these words, he turned his head in the opposite direction. His face could not be seen except the matted curly hair that hung down like vines of bitter gourd.

She raised her voice suddenly:

"You shouldn't sit here any longer. My children have fallen asleep. If you continue to sit here defiantly, I'll call Achuettan from the neighbouring house. In case he lays hands on you, not even a single bone in your body will be left unbroken."

---

* dried coconut leaves rolled into a scroll lit at one end used as a torch in villages

Suddenly he turned to look at her, and she saw his face in full for the first time. When she raised the kerosene lamp close to his face, she found it cracked and expressionless. The moment her eyes met his sunken and dim eyes she felt something crawl along her face and then slip down below. She pulled her shawl over her breast almost as a reflex action and wiped the sweat from her face with the corner of her dhoti. She paused for a moment and then whispered to him, lowering her eyes:

"Anyway, it is quite late at night, you needn't go now. You can sleep on this veranda, on condition that you will go away before dawn. If anybody asks me about you, I'll say that I didn't see you."

He turned his head again to stare into the darkness. When he sucked on the beedi hard, his cheeks stretched and sank deep into his mouth. His lips were quivering as curls of smoke rose from his mouth.

She looked at him for some time. She could hear her children snoring inside the house. The air was filled with the scent of cashew fruit. Glow worms were seen twinkling over the hedge. A dog let out a long groan somewhere near the *sarpakkavu*[**].

Remembering something, she said suddenly:

"If you are hungry, come to the west side of the house. There is some rice left in the kitchen. In case anybody happens to see you there, I'll say that you are a madman, unknown to me."

He threw away the beedi and buried his face between his legs.

** a grove where serpents are worshipped as Naga God

On second thoughts she corrected herself:

"No! Don't come to the west side. That's risky. Somebody might see you. Everybody in this locality is envious of me, just because I receive 'money orders' from my husband every month. It would be better you come into the house. But you must go away from here immediately after having the meal. You can sleep beneath the banyan tree in front of the temple or on the veranda of some shop."

He stared at her in perplexity. After a while he staggered to his feet. Loosening his dhoti, he shook it well and tied it round the waist again. Then he spat onto the courtyard. She lifted the kerosene lamp and examined his face again from a distance. That lean, sunken and dirty face was still without any expression. His shirt, drenched in sweat, was sticking to his body. He was carrying a cloth bag over his shoulder.

"Who knows the ways of today's young people? If you're hungry why don't you say it?" She murmured to herself.

After hesitating for a second, she entered the corridor with the lamp. When she reached the kitchen she turned back and saw him staring at the photograph that hung on the wall.

"That's my husband. The photo was taken immediately after our marriage. Now he has changed a lot. He's grown very grey."

His eyes slipped away from the photograph and began to crawl along the cobwebs on the wall.

"Come. It's very late and I'm sleepy," she said in a hoarse voice. He staggered into the open room adjacent to the kitchen and sat cross-legged on the black floor. She transferred the rice left in the cooking pot into a porcelain bowl and placed it before him.

"There's no curry. Can you eat it with some buttermilk and two green chillies?"

His look alternated between the rice in the bowl and his lean, cracked palm for some time. Then he raised his eyes and looked at her face. Unable to face his piercing look, she turned her face away.

"My husband will be more than happy with buttermilk, and chutney made of green chilli." She couldn't help the quiver in her voice. She licked her lips and wiped the sweat from her face with a corner of her shawl.

"What a heat! It didn't rain even on the *Sivarathri* day. My husband has written that it's very difficult for him to get leave now. Anyway, I'm sure he'll come home during the winter."

As she found nothing else to say, she fanned herself with a corner of her shawl and stared into the darkness outside the barred window. When she turned her head after some time, he was found sitting in the same posture.

Crying loudly, two cats jumped onto the courtyard from the hedge. She went close to the window and looked out. By then the cats had disappeared behind the platform of Tulsi plants.

The heat of Meenam was at a boiling point. She leaned against the window. His eyes crawled away to the bowl of rice and again returned to her face. She felt as if her shawl was slipping down because of his piercing look. A mild chill began to creep up from her toes. She felt the exhaustion from heat. Something melted inside her. She licked her dry lips, and then tried to conceal her emotions by biting the lip.

"You didn't eat anything. Aren't you hungry? Then what is it that you want?" On hearing her own hoarse voice she shuddered. She clung to the bars of the window with fatigue and invoked Lord Guruvayoorappan.

He stirred suddenly, separated his crossed legs and rose to his feet slowly, keeping one of his hands pressed to the ground for support. Staring at her once again, he lowered his weak eyes and put the cloth bag on his shoulder. Then he staggered back to the veranda.

She watched him, with her face pressed against the bars of the window.

Stepping onto the courtyard, he spat angrily on the ground and walked away with unsteady steps.

Soon his lean figure dissolved into the darkness. When he was assumed to have reached outside the gatehouse, she saw somebody coming along the alley carrying a choottu. She shuddered again.

Can the man have seen him going out of this house?

Translation of Vēnal

✦ ✦ ✦

5

A Letter from Nowhere

Sivaraman Nair was preparing basins around the banana plants when the postman Ezhuthachan came with a letter addressed to him. Cleaning his hands of the soil, he took the letter from the postman's hand and examined it, turning the sides repeatedly.

"Why master, a letter from overseas, quite unusually? Is it from Dubai?" There was a sly smile in the corner of Ezhuthachan's mouth when he asked these questions.

"Who knows, Ezhuthachan? Who is there in Dubai to write to me? Maybe from some former student," Sivaraman Nair replied with a smile.

It was an airmail envelope fringed with blue and red lines. There was a picture of an aircraft in a corner. The address was written in an unfamiliar, but clear handwriting.

"I don't think it's from any former student. Humph! Must be from somebody else...." Ezhuthachan's sharp eyes probed deep into Sivaraman Nair's face. The latter felt a little embarrassed.

After exchanging the usual pleasantries, Ezhuthachan went away. Wasting no time Sivaraman Nair opened the letter. It was the letter of one Venugopal from Qatar.

Which Venugopal? Some Venugopal has written to his father on a lined yellow piece of paper:

"We are coming. We'll reach Kochi by the first flight on the next thirteenth. 'We' means she and I. I don't have the least intention to shock you. Anyway, there's no point in repeating what has already been said several times. We have decided to live together and there's no question of changing this decision, at this point of time. As it is, just a question of either today or tomorrow, I thought it was better to have it today itself. Please talk to mother in detail and make her understand things properly."

Sivaraman Nair did not understand anything. He examined the letter again so as to get some clue about the sender. However, the sender's address was not written anywhere on the letter. Though it was mentioned to have been sent from Qatar, the postal seal was not clear.

Anyway, it is not a letter written to me. Ezhuthachan has gone; otherwise I could have given it back to him now itself.

He went through the address on the envelope once again—K. Sivaraman Nair, Keezheppadath house.... The address was exactly that of his.

Perhaps, this Venugopal is a man who knows me very well. As his love affair is a difficult matter, he may be reluctant to write about it to his father directly. Therefore he must be using me as a reliable person to tell his father about it.

But who is this Venugopal?

This was the thought in his mind while walking towards the pond in front of the house. There are only two Venugopals here whom I know well. One is Devu's husband. He's a soldier, and is somewhere in Assam now. The other one is an attendant in the veterinary hospital, and I saw him even yesterday. There may be somebody else with the same name, but I fail to remember him now.

He washed his legs and face, wiped his face well with his towel and returned to the veranda. Then he switched on the fan and sat under it. His eyes were still going through the lines of the letter.

"I saw Ezhuthachan coming here. Whose letter is it?" Janu Amma asked.

Without saying anything he handed over the letter to her. She took her spectacles from the shelf and began to read the letter in a low voice uttering each word separately. He saw an expression of bewilderment spreading on her face, and the nerves in her neck twitching.

"But whoever is this Venugopal?"

"I simply have no idea, Janu."

"If so, then Ezhuthachan must have given it to you by mistake."

"But the sender has written my address correctly."

He was lost in thought for some time. Then he added:

"Anyway, let me give it back to Ezhuthachan along with the envelope. Being the postman he visits almost all the houses in this locality. Therefore he must have some idea regarding who this Venugopal is."

Janu Amma was recollecting something. Her look alternated between the letter and her husband's face.

"You needn't give it back," she said suddenly. "Wait for two days and you will get some information."

"What information is there to get, Janu? What business we have in the family matters of a stranger called Venugopal?"

"This is not as simple as you think." Janu Amma was still scrutinising his face. "I think, there is something hidden inside."

"Hidden means...?" Sivaraman Nair stared at his wife.

"I don't know anything. Ask yourself." Walking towards the window she leaned her face against its bars and looked out.

Sivaraman Nair thought for a while. What does Janu mean? Does she believe that the letter has been written to me actually? That is to say that Venugopal is somebody known to me.

"I will give it back to Ezhuthachan tomorrow itself," he said as if to himself.

"No need of it. Try to recall things."

"What do you mean, Janu? Do you believe that I know this Venugopal?"

"I don't know. Better go back to your memories. Perhaps you may find something."

Without saying anything more, Janu Amma went to the kitchen. After a while the sound of utensils falling onto the floor was heard, together with the swearing from Janu Amma.

Suddenly, Sivaraman Nair rose to his feet. He went inside the house, changed his dress and came out with his umbrella.

"Where are you going out in this blazing heat?" Janu Amma asked as he stepped out.

"Let me seek out Ezhuthachan. He may be somewhere near the hilltop."

"You are batty," his wife muttered. "Keep the letter there. Somebody will come enquiring about it."

"Suppose nobody comes, and Venugopal arrives on the thirteenth with that girl...?"

"So what? He knows where to go. Why do you worry about it?"

"I have no worry."

Janu Amma felt a lack of confidence in his voice.

"This Venugopal has taken a very crucial decision. If his parents and relatives do not come to know of it in time...?"

"Do whatever you like. I won't say anything."—Throwing these words at her husband Janu Amma walked off.

Sivaraman Nair went out of the house. While walking in the scorching heat of Meenam under the shade of his umbrella he asked himself – Who could be this Venugopal? Why is he spiteful towards me? Why has he thrown me into this predicament?

Ezhuthachan had gone past the hill and was sitting on the platform under the banyan tree in front of the Bhagavathy Temple, chewing pan. On seeing Sivaraman Nair, who was drenched in sweat, the postman looked at him questioningly.

"Why have you come all this way in this blazing heat, master?"

"What shall I say, Ezhuthachan? You have put me in a terrible mess."

Sivaraman Nair sat on the platform beside Ezhuthachan. He wiped the sweat and fanned himself with his shawl.

"I'm returning the letter that you gave me. It is not meant for me. Give it to whoever concerned. I cannot get involved in these sorts of troubles at this age."

"What are you saying, master? It's a letter addressed to you, and I'm bound to give it to the addressee alone."

"You read the letter and then tell me whether it is intended for me or not."

However, Ezhuthachan hesitated to read the letter.

"A postman shouldn't read the letters addressed to others. The government rules are very strict. Even otherwise, as a village postman of decades, I have my reputation to keep."

"But I have already opened and read it."

"Still it's against the rule."

"If you're reluctant, let me take it out of the cover, and then you can read it without fear."

While going through the lines of the letter Ezhuthachan's eyes widened.

"It seems quite funny. I don't understand why this man has chosen you of all the people to write this kind of a letter to."

"I'm also puzzled."

Ezhuthachan spat out the tobacco refuse and thought for a while. Then he said:

"Try to recollect the past, master. It's quite clear that this Venugopal knows you well. Otherwise he wouldn't have taken such a liberty with you."

"What do you mean by saying that he knows me?" Sivaraman Nair flew into a temper. "He has called me 'father'! It's not something trivial."

"He must be one of your former students. As you have worked in a number of schools, you are sure to have students in various places."

"Do the persons whom you taught call you 'father'? What a joke!"

"Who knows? I've heard all kinds of stories about young schoolmasters working in far flung villages and living alone...."

There was a mischievous smile on Ezhuthachan's face.

Suddenly something flashed in Sivaraman Nair's head.... The peculiar expression on his wife's face.... Was she also hinting at some such possibility? He sat dazed for a while.

"What are you driving at, Ezhuthachan?'

"No, we haven't heard such things about you so far."

"What things you haven't heard?"

"I was just telling you. Don't feel bad about it, anyway. Shouldn't we think about all the possibilities regarding this kind of an issue?"

"In such a case, would I carry the letter all over? Would I show it to you, either?"

"That's also true. Even so, you just recollect your past. Is there any forgotten relationship? Some mischief committed in the prime of your life?"

"Ezhuthachan!" Sivaraman Nair screamed.

On seeing his eyes burning, Ezhuthachan was embarrassed. He took his packet of betel leaves and jumped down from the platform.

"I was just telling you. I didn't mean anything wrong...," he stammered. "What the department has asked me to do is to deliver the envelope to the addressee, and that I have done without fail. To tackle the problems caused by the contents of the letter is your responsibility."

When Ezhuthachan turned to go, the master pleaded him to stop.

"You are a regular visitor of all the houses in this locality. Just try to recollect whether there is any Venugopal from this area working in Qatar. If there is such a person it must be known to you."

"Had I known any such person, I wouldn't have put you in trouble."

Ezhuthachan smiled and rubbed the mole on his chin gently. After thinking for a while he continued:

"I've handled thousands of letters so far in my service; various kinds of letters. And now I have acquired the skill to tell you what the contents of an envelope are, by placing my finger on it. In other words, I have become one with the postal articles through the continuous acquaintance of a lifetime. We can call it a divine gift."

Sivaraman Nair remembered that it was with a peculiar expression on the face, a probing look and a sly smile in the corner of his mouth that Ezhuthachan gave him the letter.

"Anyway, what was your impression about this letter? Tell me honestly."

"Don't feel offended when I tell you frankly," Ezhuthachan hesitated for a moment.

"No problem; tell me whatever it is." Sivaraman Nair's voice wavered a little.

"My mind tells me that this letter is meant for you. And you should note that it has not been sent from abroad. It was posted from somewhere here."

As Sivaraman Nair looked at him with a bemused expression, Ezhuthachan unfolded his umbrella and walked away with a rolling gait.

Sivaraman Nair was disturbed throughout the day. He went through the lines of the letter a hundred times. The letters looked clumsy. Though he scrutinised them several times, separating and reuniting them, he could not make out anything. There were a number of gaps between the lines and between the letters. Those gaps were filled with a mysterious darkness. While groping through that thick darkness, he could hear Venugopal's laughter at a distance. A Venugopal without face. He has only fingers. Dipping those fingers in black ink he is noting down something on a yellow piece of paper; something about a strange relationship. But who is he? Who is his father? Is he searching for a father in that thick, slippery darkness? A father with a correct name, clear address and pin code? Perhaps, he does not have a father. Or his father may be against his relationship with that girl. But he believes that he must have a father's consent and blessing for a lifelong union with the girl whom he loves. Hence he looks for a person who is familiar and very dear to him, as his father. He submits everything to him and seeks his permission and blessing through a letter.

Whoever they are, they have decided to live together; and that seems a firm decision. Hence they must be prepared to face the consequences as well.

Now the only thing to be done is to bless them, keeping my hand on their heads; and wish them a happy married life.

If Venugopal had written his address in the letter, I would have sent a reply to him.

Janu Amma did not say anything. Her face looks clouded. She is brooding over something. She may be picking up all the minor incidents that have occurred during the last thirty years of their married life and trying to unravel them in a new light. Those stories that he had cooked up about his errands of bachelor days, narrated to her in the flush of youth, and the fractions of certain incidents concerning him that she heard from others must have swept back into her mind.

When she realised that he was about to ask her something, she evaded him. Thereafter, she took care to keep herself away from his presence. Hence he also withdrew into himself. In short, they were on the verge of an outburst.

Age was catching up on her. She has become too sensitive these days. Some minor issues are enough to agitate her. Then there will be fits of temper. Knowing well that it will be foolishness to try to prevent it, he evades her in such moments of outbursts. Gradually as and when everything subsides, he goes near her. Then both of them behave as if nothing has happened between them. Though they may feel some sort of unfamiliarity for some time, things will become normal soon.

He has become fed up with this drama.

While lying down at night, Sivaraman Nair kept to a side of the cot deliberately. Still he could perceive the warmth of his wife's body, a little away from him.

Closing his eyes tightly, he tried to sleep. But sleep eluded him. Pieces of yellow cloth, with black letters strewn across them, flew before his eyes; cloth pieces of different sizes and letters of various shapes and thickness.

Suddenly he felt the heat of her palm on the back of his body.

"Will you reply me if I ask you something?" Janu Amma asked in a hoarse voice.

"Yeah."

"You should tell the truth."

"Yeah."

"Where is that Padmavathy now?"

He shuddered a little and turned to lie on his back. Janu Amma moved closer to him. Her body heat had doubled. She was breathing quickly.

"How many times have I told you those things? Yet again you are pestering me with the same question!" He realised that his voice had wavered.

"You told me a lie." Janu Amma was on the verge of tears.

Sivaraman Nair did not say anything.

"After we met the doctor and did all kinds of tests, you made me believe that it was all your fault that we did not have a child."

No! Not again!

Sivaraman Nair put his fingers in his ears. He knew well the things that she would say next. Beginning with a low voice it would become louder, and lead to weeping and sobs. This had been repeated several times in the past.

Sivaraman Nair got up slowly. Going near the window he stared into the darkness outside. He could still see the pieces of yellow cloth flying in the thin darkness. He tried to pick up the black letters that remained stuck to those pieces of cloth.

"It's true that Padmavathy and I have worked together. But nothing else has happened between us as you think. I know that her husband is dead and that she has a son, working in some Gulf country. But I don't even know his name. Anyway, I don't insist that you should believe me."

"Lie! Lie!" she sobbed out sharp slivers of sound. "Then who is this Venugopal? Why has he written to you?"

"If there is anything in it as you think, I wouldn't have shown the letter to you; nor would I have gone in search of Ezhuthachan."

"Then who's this Venugopal?"

Venugopal! Sivaraman Nair stood paralysed, casting his eyes over the yellow pieces of cloth flying in the darkness.

This Venugopal could be anyone; perhaps, one whom I knew once, but have forgotten now. If not, he may be somebody who knows me. He may have chosen me as a person who would relieve him of the burden he has been bearing so far.

When his thought took such a turn, Sivaraman Nair could empathise with Venugopal. Poor boy! He has fallen in love with a girl, and they have decided to live together. Nobody can make them change that decision. Venugopal has shown at least the good sense to disclose it to his father and seek his blessing. Young people of today do not show that much sense of propriety.

If I were in that father's position? Sivaraman Nair turned his head and looked at his wife.

Lying with her face turned to the opposite direction, she was still sobbing. This time she did not burst out as usual. But she was not likely to cool down soon.

Anyway, it would not end there. Padmavathy teacher and Venugopal would linger in her mind. They would come to the surface time and again, and dance as if half-consciously.

If I were Venugopal's father, I would receive him and the girl whole-heartedly and bless them putting my hand on their heads....

He felt a choking sensation. The boy and the girl were standing before him with their heads bowed, and they were about to touch his feet so as to show their respects to him.

Had Janu given birth to a child in the normal course, I would have had a son like Venugopal, bowing before me and touching my feet like this.

Something flashed in Sivaraman Nair's head. He switched on the light.

That yellow piece of paper was lying on the table. Once again he ran his eyes over the lines written on it. Then a strange thought came to his mind.

The handwriting seems quite familiar.

Drawing a chair closer to the table he sat on it and copied the lines on another piece of paper. Then he looked at the copied lines several times, from different angles.

Thereupon a mysterious darkness clouded his mind.

The handwriting on both the pieces of paper seemed to be more or less the same.

Then he tried hard to find at least a slight difference between the two.

Translation of Katt

✦ ✦ ✦

6

The Journey

He reached the office much earlier than usual. While he was reversing the car into the parking space, the watchman came near the car and saluted him. Then he opened the door of the car for the officer to get off and took the brief case from him. As they were climbing up the stairs, the watchman cleared his throat and said:

"Anyway, you shouldn't have done this sir."

The officer did not say anything.

"It is thirty years since I joined this office. I have seen several officers during this long period. All of them were keen on getting promoted to higher posts, and they achieved their goals somehow. This is the first time an officer is simply giving up everything...."

As the officer turned his head and looked at him, the watchman swallowed his words.

There was nobody in the office except Naniyamma, the scavenger. She was cleaning the table. On seeing the officer she straightened herself up and bowed to him. There was a look of surprise on her face.

When he entered the glass cubicle provided for him, the watchman switched on the light and fan.

After a while he looked at himself in the mirror, kept in the resting room. No, my face has not changed. It is the same expressionless face. As I went on drinking late in the night yesterday, the eyelids have swollen a little. I can't remember the youngster's face that was seen in the mirror when I entered this room for the first time, ten years ago. That youngster, however, had long curly hair and a thick moustache. He was capable of smiling sweetly. Within the past ten years, his hair has thinned just like the seashore from where waves have retreated. The tangled strands of hair that remain on either side of the head have an ugly copper colour.

He came back to the cubicle and sat on the chair. The empty file-tray was still there on the table. 'Even the last paper presented before me was cleared yesterday. Now I am free of all the obligations to the company,' he thought.

Seshayyar reached earlier than usual. His forehead was painted with sacred ash and vermilion. Basil leaves were tucked behind his ears.

"Good morning, sir!"

"Good morning!"

"I am coming from the temple, sir." Putting a leaf bowl on the table he added, "Here is the prasadam."

"That's good, especially because today is a good day for you."

"I want your blessing, sir." He shut his eyes and bowed low to the officer.

"What are you doing, Swamy?" the officer expressed his annoyance at seeing a man older than him bending his head before him.

"I don't know whether your shoes will fit me well, sir. So..."

"That's a baseless doubt, Swamy. Anybody's shoes will fit anybody, provided you have a liking for them."

Swamy's forehead seemed to be sweating.

"Come and sit here on this chair, Swamy. I will sit on some other chair."

"No, sir. I'll occupy that chair only after your leaving this office. Besides, it is to be ensured that shifting to that chair is done at an auspicious moment."

The officer leaned back in the revolving chair and lit a cigarette.

"Let me ask you something, sir..." Swamy hesitated for a while and added, "what made you take this kind of a decision so suddenly?"

"It's not a sudden decision. I had been thinking about it for a long time."

"Any better job offered?"

"No."

Sheshayyar did not ask anything more.

'Ten years in various places and then another ten years here. I should have got rooted in the company within this time. The chairman also said it at the farewell dinner yesterday. When I said that I can't get rooted anywhere, the chairman said, patting on my back: "You drink too much."'

When the clock struck ten, the staff came to the office one by one. They gathered round the glass cubicle, without knowing what to ask or tell him. He looked at them and smiled.

After a while the union leader came to the cubicle and sat on the opposite chair.

"We are very much sorry that you are leaving the company; that too at such young an age, giving up a good career. It's a big loss to our organisation. Our matters were quite safe in your hands."

The officer tried to smile. The chairman's words rang in his head: 'You were a shrewd executive. It's not an easy thing to win the favour of the company and the labour at once. Your's was a superb performance. Anyhow, tell me frankly what made you take this decision. If you are desirous of better terms, don't hesitate to reveal it.'

'No such desires, sir. Just as you are not born as a chairman, I'm not born as an executive. We all reached here somehow. We represent a new class of authorities created by competitive examinations. It is very difficult to climb up. Climbing down seems quite easy.'

The union leader too wanted to know the reason. Clasping his hands behind his head and giving out a yawn, the officer answered him in just a sentence:

"I'm fed up."

The leader stared at him as if he did not understand what the officer said. Swamy stood open-mouthed. The sacred ash and vermilion on his forehead were drenched in sweat.

After some time everything became normal. The crowd dispersed and retreated to their respective chairs. The typewriters and telephones began to make sound. People were coming into and going out of the office. Everything was as usual; the same monotonous repetition of things. The officer dozed off for some time. Various scattered and sliding pictures came into his dream. When he woke up suddenly after a while, he found that seated on the opposite chair Swamy was staring at him. There was a bewildered look on his face.

"Do you feel unwell, sir? Swamy asked.

"No."

"I was just thinking... I don't have as much proficiency in English as that of you. Anyway, it is just because of your decision to resign that I have got a promotion in this old age. I have just two more years left in my service."

The officer looked at the watch. There was not much time left. Swamy must be eager to sit on this chair, although he pretended otherwise. I didn't have any right to keep him waiting endlessly. This was quite a natural change.

He began to write a letter to his son, who was studying at a boarding school far away.

"At this age you cannot understand me. When I say that I was quite bewildered without knowing how to find out the distance between the points A and B, you will laugh. At your age, however, the same question perplexed me. If you have never felt so, that perplexing moment is yet to come. You will be able to understand me then. Goodbye!"

Now one more thing remained to be done. He turned the pages of his diary hurriedly.

'I have noted his number somewhere in the diary. Where is it? I have forgotten his name... What is it? Balachandran, Ramachandran, Ramakrishnan, or Raveendran....?' He scratched his head.

'Yes, it is Ramachandran.' After searching for a long time he found out the telephone number.

The voice at the other end was a bit tired.

"Isn't it Mr. Ramachandran?"

"Yes."

"I'm K. R. Nair."

"Who?"

"Santha's husband."

"Oh."

"Can you come to my house at noon today? Let's have lunch together."

"I'm a little busy today. Can't we have it some other day?"

"No. I've some important matters to tell you."

"Let me try to come."

"You must come. It's a very important matter."

"I have..."

"Santha has asked me to request you on her behalf as well."

"Okay, I'll come."

"Thank you!"

The officer put the telephone down, feeling much relieved. Then he lit a cigarette.

The blue envelope with the company's stamp lay on the table. It contained the chairman's letter expressing gratitude for serving the company for a long period. He had expressed regret that the company would not get my service henceforth. The company would be deeply indebted to me for the hard work rendered during its developmental stage. There's a cheque for a great amount too in the envelope—the final settlement! They must have struck my name off their thick account book, using a red inked pen; and must have noted in the margin— 'resigned from the company on 13th July.'

Reason?

'What is the reason shown in the resignation letter? I don't remember it. Have I written repeatedly that I'm fed up?'

He rose from the chair and bade farewell to everybody with his palms put together in namaskar.

Swamy escorted him to the car. When they shook hands at the parting moment, Swamy said:

"Whenever I need your help I will contact you, sir. Will you please give me your contact number?"

"My contact number?" the officer laughed. The only number known to me henceforth will be my date of birth."

Swamy's eyes seemed getting wet with tears.

The scorching sun had melted the tar on the road. While driving the car he was thinking about Ramachandran. 'Won't he come? Can he ignore my words about santha's request?'

Instead of taking to the shed he parked the car in the yard. Santha came running on hearing the calling bell. Her eyes were red from crying.

He put his hand on her shoulder and took it back suddenly. While changing clothes he said:

"Get me a drink."

Ice cubes were floating in the frothy soda.

Santha's sobbing was heard from the bedroom. He did not think it necessary to console her. This was a natural transition. Nobody needed to feel pained. It should have happened much earlier.

He dozed off again.

When he opened his eyes he found Santha sitting on the sofa opposite to him. She had washed and powdered her face; had applied eyeliner and was dressed up in a smooth silk sari. She was staring at him. He looked her up and down, and said:

"Now you look like a beautiful bride. Good! So you have understood things at last."

She did not say anything; but there was a frozen expression on her face.

"Ramachandran will come to have lunch with us. At first he tried to refuse the invitation; but he agreed to come when I lied that you had asked me to convey your special request to him."

She continued to remain silent with the same frozen expression.

He filled the glass again.

'I must finish this bottle, because Ramachandran does not drink.' He thought.

"I've written to our son," he said without looking at her face.

While sitting at the dining table Ramachandran's face looked pale. He looked incredulously at the faces of Santha and her husband alternately.

"There's nothing to disbelieve in it," Santha's husband said. "She told me everything in the beginning of our married life. She cheated you. Just like any other girl in such trying situation, what she preferred was a secure life. Hence she decided to marry me. She could forget you quite easily; but you wasted your life like an idiot, burying yourself in the memories about her. Anyway, now I am giving her to you. Forgive me for using her so far."

"Mr. Nair..."

"I was preparing myself for this handover, for a long time. I never thought it would be so easy to cut off everything. I've settled all the accounts I can remember. Are there some more obligations left to be fulfilled? Who knows? What a short memory we all have!"

"But... I...."

"Please don't say 'no'. I have procured everything required for Santha to live comfortably—a house, a car, a son, the amount I received from the company, an insurance policy and above all, you. No, she won't have any difficulty in life."

Unable to face his eyes, Ramachandran stared at Santha's face; but he could not find any particular expression there. She was eating greedily like one who had been starving.

Her husband continued:

"Years ago, while studying at school, a mathematical problem perplexed me very much. The teacher asked us to mark two points on a piece of paper and to find out the distance between the two. The other students said that it could be found out easily using a ruler; but I sat there staring at the two points in bewilderment. The distance between two points can be anything. You can start from 'A' and take a roundabout course to reach 'B', wandering wherever you can. Then how will you find out the correct distance? As a crow is likely to take different courses while flying from one place to another, the distance covered by it will not be the same always."

"I don't understand," Ramachandran muttered.

"That's a great blessing. You can give Santha a life devoid of worries and cares."

He rose from the chair belching loudly and washed his hand.

"Am I to do anything more? Don't hesitate to ask."

Ramachandran sat with his face bent. It seemed that he was yearning to say something.

Santha was still seated at the dining table, with the same expressionless face. Her fingers were moving in the plate mechanically.

Her husband walked into the bedroom and came out soon wearing an old torn shirt and a dirty dhoti. He stood for a few seconds at the front door and said without turning his head:

"So, let me go."

Stepping onto the road that was burning hot, he walked away without causing his footprints to be stamped in the melted tar.

Translation of Yātra

7

Swamy

Swami sat in between two corpulent persons in a safari suit, with his face drooped. The table in front of them was covered with a red table cloth with various pictures printed on it. A few incense sticks were burning in a holder kept on the table. Bits of ashes resembling scales of fish were hanging from their tips.

The man on the left side of Swamy whispered:

"So, let's begin Swamy?"

Swamy simply nodded.

The hall was crowded with people. Most of them were Swamy's fellow workers. A few customers were also there as special invitees. Besides, there was a youngster carrying a camera over his shoulder.

The man who whispered to Swamy rose to his feet and smiled at the audience. Somebody ran onto the dais and adjusted the height of the mike.

"The function begins with an invocation to God."

All the people in the hall stood up.

A girl in a green skirt came forward from the front row of the audience and recited a verse in a quavering voice, with a little stage fright. When she finished the recitation somehow, she gave a smile of relief and ran back to her seat. The man who announced the commencement of the function stood up again and grinned at the audience. Then he cleared his throat and began to speak with commendable ease:

"Our Swamy is leaving after being with us for a long period of forty-three years. That means, Swamy came here while I was studying in the Montessori school; the time when my grandfather, the senior Lalaji opened a small agency office here. He is one of the first few employees of this group of companies that has become a great business empire today. I can imagine the senior Lalaji and Swamy seated before their tables in a small room. I have heard it said that Swamy had an amazing ability to perceive each and every pulse of senior Lalaji's mind. They thought together, dreamt together and made the correct moves together. Do you know how many places this man had visited as the sole representative of the senior Lalaji, particularly during the times when the war became fierce? In those days travel facilities were limited. Besides, Swamy was very young and was just a matriculate. He was unable to speak English fluently. Still he turned out to be a great success wherever he went. As you could imagine, in those days Swamy had to work day and night. He would be able to go to sleep only around midnight. Hence, he slept in the office itself the blessed little room where our companies took root and flourished. In memory of the senior Lalaji his old chair has been still kept in that room."

Swamy was listening to the speech carefully. The MD's words rippled over his head. Memories rushed into his mind. What appeared first on his mind's screen was his first meeting with the senior Lalaji. He had just eaten a meagre meal served in a cracked bowl when his *periyappa* took him to Lalaji's house. The Lalaji looked at Swamy's sunken eyes and the torn shirt. It could be read from his face that he was not impressed with the boy. Swamy's periyappa realised it and said repeatedly: "My grandson is a brilliant boy, Lalaji. He would always score cent percent in mathematics. But we can't afford to send him to Kochi for higher studies. That's why I've brought him over here. Just pay him whatever you please. The conditions at our house are so miserable." Lalaji stared into Swamy's eyes, as if trying to pick something from them. Periyappa seemed to have realised it. Hence he added quickly: "You can trust him Lalaji. Poor though we are, ours is a dignified family. He is capable of becoming a Professor, in case he gets the opportunity for higher education. He can continue his studies while staying here, if you desire so." Lalaji smiled. What he wanted was an obedient and faithful assistant, who would never divulge any of his secrets. Hence Swamy's education ended there. But he learned a great many things related to business.

After drinking a mouthful of water the MD continued:

"I needn't tell you anything about Swamy's wonderful accounting sense, because you all know it well. You must have experienced his amazing memory power as well. Years back, when there was a discussion about installing a computer in the head office, I said jocularly: 'There's a wonderful man in one of our companies about a thousand miles away. Let's bring him over here and keep in a glass cage so that we can save the cost and the maintenance expenses of a minicomputer. As he is an intelligent and prudent human being, he'll be more reliable as well'."

The audience laughed loudly. What the MD said was true. Swamy remembered that some of his fellow workers used to call him 'Computer Swamy'; some of them teasingly, and the others enviously. Though I worked here for the last so many years, I haven't even touched a small machine. The young employees of today require a calculator even for adding five and three. In my case, numbers in different shapes and colours have always been my companions. Each number has its own distinct face, behaviour and movements. While sitting languidly on that old chair in the office the mind slips automatically into meditation. When the entire self withdraws into some unknown point, I can hear the music of numbers and their rhythmic dance with effortless and well controlled steps. An illusory ring of soft threads knitted together as done by a spider.... When I spoke about it to my fellow workers, they laughed at it. They couldn't see the faces of numbers; nor could they hear their rhythm and believe that they too have a life.... "Swamy has no life outside the office. He works there till midnight, and that's why he experiences such hallucinations," somebody said. I didn't counter it; simply smiled without saying anything. Even as many things slipped out of my hands, I curled up within that soft net.

Lalaji himself had asked one day: "Shouldn't there be a change in your life? Don't you want somebody to share your life?"

On hearing these words I looked at him incredulously. I hadn't thought about such things till then. Though my days are busy, there are not many worries and cares. Then why should there be an entanglement? This was my line of thinking. However, Lalaji brought up the matter again after a few days: "Isn't it good to have somebody waiting to see you back at home after a busy day's work? A homely woman to serve you supper, wash your clothes and sleep with you?" I didn't feel anything in particular. But as it was asked by Lalaji I nodded as usual. That was how Alamelu had come into my life quite unexpectedly. Her parents had died years ago. And she didn't know much about the world.

The MD continued:

"... I cannot but reveal certain things on this occasion. During the critical phases of the development of our companies, representatives of various foreign companies used to visit us to discuss new projects. There would be some cunning consultants with them. They would try to trap us by throwing certain complicated jargons at us. In such trying situations my father and I would manage to escape from their tricky ways and withdraw into the adjacent anteroom. Swamy would be sitting there. He would lead us through all those shortcuts, of which we couldn't even guess. The ease with which Swamy suggested ways for handling such knotty situations was something astounding even to me, despite my studies and trainings abroad related to Business Management. Above all academic qualifications, there is something known as practical knowledge, derived from experience. You can call it native intelligence."

Now Swamy was lost in some other memory; the memory of an accursed Saturday.

A red-complexioned European had come to the company to discuss some business deal. The talks extended into the second day. While the ceaseless discussions were going on after lunch, I got the information that Alamelu had been hospitalised. It was her second successive abortion. She was taken to the hospital in a taxi by some of our neighbours. As she lay there bathed in blood, the neighbours themselves ran here and there to procure the rare type of blood required for her treatment. All this while, Lalaji was bargaining hard with the European. When the second phone call came, Lalaji said: "Don't worry, Swamy. I'll send Suresh with my car to the hospital. He'll manage everything as our own man. He is very efficient. When the third call came within half an hour, Lalaji didn't tell me anything. He was heard mentioning the name of some doctor to his secretary through the intercom. The discussions hadn't reached anywhere. The European was to leave for Delhi in the evening flight. He wanted to visit Taj Mahal the next day and to return the day after. What came next was not any phone call, but the P.R.O. Suresh himself. Squeezing my hand, he patted my back consolingly.... I can just remember entering the hospital room, propped up by somebody. When the white cloth was removed from her face I could see the face a little swollen, but it was quite calm; the calmness that manifested the relief she felt after having suffered a lot of pain. Later on, during some nights, Alamelu, covered in white cloth, appeared in my sleep. She was not crying. There was no particular expression on her face. The same submissive look that was on her face while paying obeisance to me by touching my feet on the first night of our marriage; and the reflection of the sob that remained suppressed inside her from childhood onwards, caused by the feeling that she had no one to be considered her own....

The MD had wound up his speech. Some other higher officials also spoke after him. All of them were born after my joining the company. They have passed great examinations. They all praised me unnecessarily. Their words of consolation and pieces of advice regarding how to make future life prosperous were all hollow and insincere.

Swamy felt something surging up inside him and an unknown pain underneath. He writhed in the chair.

Suddenly Swamy found Alamelu slowly coming forward through the middle of the hall, pushing aside the people on her way. Her hair was untied and falling loose. She was wearing loose, thin white clothes. Stains of blood were seen on her undergarment.

Stepping closer, she stood before him looking intently at his face. Her face had always been quite expressionless, without even a shade of complaint. But now for the first time Swamy found a sad expression in her eyes. Her dry lips were quivering. Those lips seemed to ask several questions silently.

Is it for this, for being seated tiredly like this with your head and body bent, in front of your superiors, that you melted away a whole life? The same questions that lay hidden from me behind the thick covering that she always put on her face, while I was writhing in the armchair with severe pain caused by the bleeding piles. Why, why are you spoiling your life? But she never asked any such question; nor did she ask for anything. There was a frightened look on her face always.

"Are you okay, Swamy?" the Director on the right side asked in a soft voice.

Swamy shook his head.

"It's all right. This is an occasion when anybody in Swamy's position will become emotional," the MD said. "But Swamy is not leaving us, because we want him forever."

Bottles containing a cold yellow liquid and paper plates with some biscuits and dry fruits were placed before the guests.

Somebody was still making a speech. Swamy's mind slipped into memories again. I missed Alamelu just for five or six days. Presently, I was back in the office again; in the same old room, on a newly bought revolving chair. "Paying more attention to your work is the easiest way to get out of your personal problems," Lalaji used to say.

But now, when Alamelu stands in front of the gathering and stares into my eyes, I feel exhausted. Questions are piling up on her face; hundreds of pointed questions. For the first time she is trying to force a reply out of me. While she was alive, she hadn't asked for anything; nor had she expressed any desire.

One day she said: "I must predecease you; if not, I'll have to trace the roots of some broken relationships and become a burden to somebody, or to drag my life in some home for the destitute."

Anyhow, that desire of hers was fulfilled; she could go away before me, without leaving any family ties.

However, I missed her just for five or six days. Then... then everything became just as they were. I was back again in the same rented flat with two rooms; the same old stove and 'ever silver' utensils; and the stench of dirty clothes.

"Swamy didn't eat anything," the MD reminded him.

Swamy simply shook his head.

"Have some cool drink at least, Swamy. Your throat must be parched."

It was time for the function to be ended. The MD stood up and said: "Now for Swamy's response."

But Swamy didn't stir from his chair. He looked around in perplexity as if startled out of a nap. He realised that everybody present in the hall was now looking at him.

Alamelu is still there in the very centre of the hall; in the same posture, and keeping her eyes fixed on his face. She is awaiting a reply from her husband.

Her eyes are cruel now. There's an unfamiliarity which was not there before. She is raising her hand slowly and pointing at me.

Swamy felt that a wooden deck has been erected around him all of a sudden. Placing a thick book before him, somebody makes him keep his hand on it and take oath... what I'm going to tell is the truth, nothing but the truth.

The MD touches Swamy lightly on his back and whispered in his ears: "Speak at least a few words, Swamy, for courtesy's sake. They're all waiting."

The MD realised that a perplexed look had taken over Swamy's face. The sandal paste on Swamy's forehead was soaked in sweat. Even though the room was cool, his shirt drenched in sweat was sticking to his body.

"Say a few words, Swamy; about Lalaji, whom these people haven't seen; and about the company."

Alamelu's forefinger seems to lengthen towards me. Her face is light red in colour. The vermilion put just below the hair has slipped onto the forehead. The big decorative mark on the forehead is glowing. She is waiting for a reply Why did you spoil your life? What for?

Swamy felt tired. Though he tried hard to rise to his feet, he collapsed into the chair. The sweat was pouring off him. He felt the coldness rushing through his nerves. Some things surged up from his stomach and he felt sourness in his mouth. Below, at the very bottom he experienced a burning sensation and a severe pain.

I must speak something, because it is the MD who is demanding me... I have never failed him in the past....

When Swamy staggered to his feet, he felt a numbness rising from the soles of his feet. His muscles were paralysed.

Two red-hot spear heads are darting towards me from Alamelu's face. She is blazing with fury.

"Oh God, blood!" somebody exclaimed.

When Swamy stood up, his seat was found covered in blood.

Somebody held Swamy so as to protect him from falling.

When water was sprinkled onto his face, Swamy opened his eyes. He found many perplexed and anxious faces around him.

"I... I have nothing to say, Sir," Swamy said in a hoarse voice. "During the last so many years it was you all who spoke to me and I have been just a listener. And now I don't find anything to tell you...."

His words ended up as a deep sob.

Translation of Sāmi

✦ ✦ ✦

8

A Tale of Two Cities

That day when Viswanathan returned home from his office it was very late and extremely dark. His wife Ragini who was very worried had by then called up many people she knew enquiring about him.

His shirt was drenched in sweat. While hanging it on the hook he said to his wife:

"Though we have been living in this city for so long, it's only today I came to know that there are so many by-ways here through which we could ride our scooter."

"What happened?"

"A major part of the old city has been barricaded and kept under guard by the police. Policemen have been posted at the many entrances to the new city as well. Hence I had to take a difficult and roundabout way to reach here somehow."

"What is the matter?"

"Some incidents are going on in the old city."

"But it is not even the festival season."

"We are capable of converting any season into a festival."

"Still, at this unexpected time...!"

"This intriguing unexpectedness may also be a peculiarity of our city; and it may have a particular pattern as well."

"What is the cause this time?"

"It's the same old dirty tricks. The malicious scribbling that somebody hurls into the sky comes back as ten-fold, hundred-fold or thousand-fold...."

"Luckily, our Raju has returned home in time," Ragini said, running her fingers through her son's curly hair."

"His school is in the new city. On the other side there is the old city, a kind of sore thumb that may swell any moment," he said while entering the bathroom.

Later on, while sitting at the dining table, he could notice a strange excitement on his son's face.

"I've heard that there was a firing in the old city; but have no idea, how many people turned stiff," said Raju.

"No, son," Ragini affectionately held him close to her. "Good children shouldn't talk like that. Who knows when and where such incidents will take place?"

"It is always so," Viswanathan said. "The dishonesty of bullets begins there. The names of the chests into which they should pierce through are never written on the bullets."

"The points of knives are also ignorant of the marks on the chests of the victims."

While Viswanathan was chewing and swallowing bread and scrambled eggs, the dark memories of some festival seasons in the past came to Ragini's mind.

"What are you thinking, Ragini?"

"About the festivals...."

"And the preparations for war behind them as well," he added.

The son did not show any interest in that conversation and he switched on the TV.

"Let's hear the news," Raju said.

His parents were surprised; because it was the first time their son was switching on the TV for watching the news.

His mother rubbed his cheek gently with an immense sense of pride.

When the girl who was reading the news said with a grim voice that curfew had been imposed in the old city, Ragini was watching her with interest.

"The new sari matches you well, Surekha," Ragini said.

"I'm Sujatha, and not Surekha," The newsreader corrected Ragini from the glass screen. "It has been brought from *Rasal khaima* by Unniyettan's elder brother. Is it good, sister?"

"It suits your complexion extremely well. Try to obtain matching earrings as well."

"Thanks, sister."

Sujatha returned quickly to news-reading. While giving the information that a part of the old city was on fire, she lowered her voice considerably. She reported that while the police and the firefighters were trying hard to put out the fire in one area, it was spreading rapidly over another. However, she assured repeatedly that still the situation was perfectly under control. As Ragini felt that there was something wrong in that assurance, she asked:

"Tell me the truth, Sujatha. How many people have died actually?"

"I'll lose my job if I disclose the truth, sister," Sujatha said with a frightened expression. "I have heard it said on the verandah that the death toll is around twenty. But we have been instructed to report it to be five. One fell into the gutter while fleeing; another was crushed under a truck; the third died of suffocation and cardiac arrest when he was caught in a stampede; and the fourth ...."

"Enough. Enough. At least you will admit there were a couple of firings!"

"But we didn't hear any sound, sister. You know, the studio is sound proof. Even otherwise, how can we distinguish the sound of firing in this city where firecrackers explode always?"

When Sujatha turned the pages and moved on to Kampuchea, Viswanathan heaved a sigh of relief.

"Our city was not like this before, Viswam," Ragini said.

"No city was like this before."

"What happened to our city?"

"Something wrong has occurred to all cities."

"It seems our city has lost its soul."

"Which city has a soul, Ragini?"

At that moment Sujatha drew their attention with a news flash.

"Here is a piece of news received just now. The army has been readied to be deployed in the old city. They will stage a flag march along the important roads tomorrow. Orders have been issued to the effect that each soldier in uniform can shoot and kill any number of people."

Then, looking at a scroll of paper that bore the government stamp, she began to read out the instructions to the public:

"People should remain vigilant at all times. If any malicious writings happen to reach your hands, burn it immediately. Be careful not to go into the streets whenever curfew is imposed.

Those who live in tall buildings should not stick their heads out of the windows opening to the street, because stray bullets may take anybody's life. And finally, don't buy stolen goods, even if they are offered at very low prices. Instead, report the matter to the nearest police station."

"The same things have been repeating for many years now! Why, even the colour of this scroll of paper has been always the same light red!" Viswanathan said. "It all begins from some malicious writings by invisible fingers. Thereafter underground forces take control of everything. All the shops in the bazaar may be remaining with their hearts cleaved now. The costly goods in those shops are being carried away to various places across the boundaries."

There was an anxious look on Sujatha's face now.

"You look worried; what is wrong, Surekha?"

"Not Surekha; Sujatha," she corrected Ragini again, sadly. "Everybody makes mistakes about my name. Why sister? Don't I have the look of a Sujatha?"

"Yes, you have it in abundance, girl," Ragini assured her. "But now your face looks tense."

"My daughter! I don't know whether she has returned home from school," Sujatha said hesitantly. "Her school is in the boundary between the two cities. It is Unniyettan who fetches her whenever the buses are not plying. Today he will have to go round the entire old city to fetch her...."

Ragini could understand Sujatha's anxiety.

"When I called Unniyettan's office nobody picked up the phone," Sujatha added in a quavering voice.

"Why can't you go home and see whether your daughter has reached there?"

"There's one more news-reading after two hours, sister. According to the rule I can go home only after it."

On thinking about the tension that Sujatha would have to suffer between the two readings, Ragini suggested:

"Shall we look around, Viswam? Poor Sujatha! She doesn't have anybody to help her."

But Viswanathan pretended that he had not heard her.

Thereafter, while giving a detailed report on Bosnia, Sujatha's sorrow crossed all bounds. She sniffed frequently and rubbed her parched throat gently with her fingers.

Ragini's son was not amused. He said:

"She is making all those ridiculous gestures on the screen! Doesn't she know that so many people are watching her?"

"Mothers alone can understand another mother's anxiety," Ragini declared.

In the mean time, a friend had checked up over the phone whether Viswanathan had reached home. It was one Makhija, living in a narrow street in the old city. His voice revealed that he was enjoying the evening with a couple of drinks.

"At this rate the curfew will continue at least for three more days, Viswam," Makhija said. "Hence I am going to stay put in my house for those three days, without bothering the least about the world outside. Life will be very boring if you don't get intervals like this occasionally; especially when you are having a nice time that your wife gifted to you by being away at her mother's in connection with her delivery."

When Sujatha finished news-reading and disappeared from the glass screen Ragini switched off the TV and sat on the chair.

"Poor girl! I can't bear to see her anguish," she said.

"Many people in this city must be suffering similar sorrows now."

"Still the sorrow that you see before your eyes is always more intense."

"That must be the reason why TV channels are flourishing in our country. The TV screens are full of grief."

Ragini turned her back on Viswanathan as if expressing her dislike of his comment. But after a while she continued:

"Will the old sorrows of the old city begin to disturb the calm of our new city as well, Swami?"

"The distinction such as old and new becomes irrelevant in case of sorrow. Still, with plenty of open space, air and light, people living in the new cities, should be capable of keeping away from such black magic; at least in their minds. While running frantically for amassing more and more worldly possessions, how can they find time to keep the old accounts in mind?"

"It's true, Viswam." Ragini nodded.

"The old city with its centuries' old forts, walls and tombs suffocate me.... Darkness and the stale smell of decay dwelling among the mossy and mouldy pieces of laterite stone."

"The senseless souls that wander about through the surfaces of those tombs seek new bodies in order to settle certain old scores."

"That itself is the reason why it seems high time we cut the two cities away."

"Old cities remain as memories, Ragini."

"True. The new cities, on the other hand, do not carry the load of memories."

At the same time, Viswanathan was thinking about the impossibility of separating the new city from the old one.

The two cities with their old and new histories are so much intertwined that they can never be cut into two. Anyhow, what history is there for the new cities to tell?

He settled himself in the armchair longing to sit for a while with his eyes closed. But at that very moment his son inserted into his computer a new disc containing some clamorous science fiction. The huge flying saucers that roar along the sky land suddenly onto grasslands and the narrow valleys between mountains, causing the areas to quake. Through the clouds of dust and pieces of grass that rise high in the air some robotic creatures wearing peculiar metal shields are sliding down. Moving their mechanical legs and hands they are advancing rapidly. The wind is howling. The soil is getting loose. The earth is splitting here and there. Huge rocks are rolling down the mountain slopes. The glass screen is full of magnetic waves.

Viswanathan sat in his chair, grinding his teeth and putting his fingers in his ears.

"Don't disturb your father, darling; turn the volume down," Ragini advised her son.

But the son did not seem to have heard it. He was trying to imitate the movements of the creatures from the outer space, quite excitedly. Then the mother herself turned the volume down, causing sparks of protest on the son's face.

"You elders don't know anything. These things can be enjoyed only if they are heard in high volume," he screamed.

Viswanathan too felt it to be true. For each action there should be a matching background sound and a decibel level. For each throat a matching gun; for each bullet that rips through the air there are separate war cries whose meanings are unknown.

He rose to his feet slowly and went onto the barred balcony in order to escape from the sounds coming from the computer. At that time the streets below were very quiet. The yellow lights of the night had already been switched on. People were walking leisurely under the lamp posts, biting off grains of millet. A mother was pushing a perambulator with her baby seated in it. Her husband was seen behind her talking loudly to somebody over his mobile phone. Some sales girls were walking hurriedly along the edge of the road to the bus station, cracking jokes.

No, nothing has happened to this city.... Viswanathan tried to console himself. In a sense what Ragini said is true. That bad city, with a number of unwanted memories lurking in it, should be cut away.

The roars of the robots is still heard clearly in the living room. It seems that Ragini also has joined her son in enjoying the scenes on the computer screen. Her laughter has filled the room. She can laugh and cry like children even at this age. That's good, anyway. She can forget the old city and the sad face of Sujatha, at least for a short while.

The phone rang at that moment. Viswanathan took the remote. It was Makhija again. His slurred speech revealed that he was quite high. It seemed as though he was holding a glass in his hand.

Makhija said that he was standing on the open terrace at the top of their old building. He was talking like an expert commentator, and repeated several times that the terrace he was standing on was the best point to see clearly the present spectacles in the old city.

"It is a spectacle of a lifetime, Viswam!" Makhija said, brimming with happiness. He was trying hard to pull out his words that had sunk into intoxication. "While standing on top of this six-storied building, our old city looks like a gypsies' valley with so many tents in it. Kitchen fires are burning all around. The streets are reverberating with angry shouts and challenges in various languages. Some people are seen running. Do you want to hear the clamour?

Here it is...."

When Makhija held the phone in the direction of the street with a loud laughter, Viswanathan could hear even the distant sounds of isolated firings.

"Did you hear it well, my friend?"

"I heard it," Viswanathan muttered. He was eager to put the phone down.

"That is firing by our policemen. It must be for the first time in your life that you hear it..."

"Yeah..."

"Tomorrow perhaps we may be lucky enough to hear the sound of the army guns."

Suddenly Viswanathan thought of warning him.

"Your standing in the open at this time is dangerous, Makhija. You'd be better going inside."

"What danger?" He laughed aloud. "You call yourselves the Lord of the World and still scared of these crackers on the ground. It is surprising! When shall we get another opportunity to see such spectacles live? Since you cannot see it with your own eyes you won't get the thrill, however picturesque a commentary I could give you. When I did not want to miss this opportunity of passing it on to some of my close friends, your number came first, and luckily got the connection too. You see, I was trying the number of this wretched cousin of mine in Canada for long. He is not picking up the phone. Possibly sleeping...."

Even though Viswanathan was trying hard to shake off those inhuman words, he repeated the warning:

"Be careful, Makhija."

"Careful about what?"

"These mischievous bullets flying into the air have neither eyes nor ears. Once out in the open they enjoy going astray. Have you ever thought of the freedom of a bullet leaving a rogue gun... touch wood!"

Viswanathan shuddered for a moment and touched the window sill in front of him.

"That's where you are mistaken." Makhija roared with laughter. "Our police cannot shoot even a stork properly; let alone me standing in the sky...."

At that moment Viswanathan felt Makhija's voice rising higher into the sky. He must be seeking higher vantage points from where he will get more and more distant spectacles required for his commentary.

When the sound of a big explosion was heard over the phone, it seemed to be as rough as that of a firecracker. Viswanathan realised that the old city was now sinking into a number of very primitive sounds. Suddenly he felt a peculiar coldness crawling up his toe. He withdrew his leg with the disgust of having trodden on a snake. Then he put the phone down.

"Who is it?" Ragini had come near him by then.

"A friend of mine, one Makhija, who lives in the old city. He says he is watching and enjoying the incidents in the street, standing on top of a six-storied building. He is also trying to give a faithful running commentary of what he sees to his friend, over the telephone."

"How strange!"

"How cruel!"

"In his eyes those tragic and terrific sights are nothing different from what you see during a *Pooram* festival. Most often this is the way a city looks at happenings, Ragini."

Having remembered something suddenly, Ragini said:

"By the way, a wonderful thing happened a little while ago. I called you from the storeroom several times, but you didn't hear."

"I was here on this balcony...."

"Do you remember the Saturday on which we came to this rented house for the first time? How hard we worked that day to clean this house! The tenants from Vijayawada who had lived here before our occupying this house had left a lot of rubbish here. We had to spend half a day for removing it. I got a dusty photograph from that rubbish. When it was cleaned well the picture of a girl wearing a Churidar was revealed. A girl of about sixteen years of age with a pretty face, sparkling eyes and a big mole on the chin."

Viswanathan nodded his head as if he could recollect everything about the photograph.

"When you insisted that the photograph should not be thrown away I told you to avoid such finds as far as possible, because that was not the first of such instances."

"I don't know why, I couldn't throw it away then; the photo of a girl whom I have never seen! Finding no space to hang it, I had put it aside several times. But on all such occasions I felt her eyes following me. In those days, I could see the mole on her chin even in my sleep. Those eyes, that looked stricken, seemed to beg for something. At last, I found a little space for her on the wall of the storeroom."

Viswanathan stared at her with disbelief; whereas Ragini's eyes were becoming wider and wider. It made him think that she was straying alone through some spectacles of her own, which he could not see.

After a while Ragini continued:

"She talked to me today from that wall.... Just a little while ago.... For a long time...," she stammered. She didn't know how to convince him.

Viswanathan laughed silently.

"So you have come out with some new eccentricities, or rather meaningless thoughts! It was various creatures and plants that used to talk to you so far. Now it is an old photo that is getting eaten by white ants!"

"This is not eccentricity, Viswam." Ragini raised her voice. "I really heard her voice. It was delicate like the sound of a *thamburu*. Perhaps, I saw her with new eyes today. Her face seemed to be one that I saw among a crowd at some festival venue years ago. She thanked me for providing her some space in this house, instead of throwing away in the rubbish dump. It was with a sob that she said she cannot go away from this house."

Viswanathan shrugged his shoulder. There was no smile on his face now. It showed more fear rather than perplexity.

"So there is yet another unwanted presence in our house!" he muttered.

Ragini did not seem to have heard it. She continued with excitement:

"What she told me, too, was something related to a festival season. At an evening like this she was running here and there in a burning city, having lost her way. She was returning from college with her friends. But the mad crowd in the city caused them to disperse in different directions, and the girl was left alone to experience all the terrors of such a situation. There was not even a single lamplight in the entire area. The footsteps of those who were running along the road, which was trembling in the darkness, parted their way into different byroads. She, too, ran into such a byroad...."

Ragini stopped there. She felt hoarseness of the throat. Her eyes were filled with tears.

Viswanathan said in a subdued voice:

"Never preserve such photos, Ragini."

"Why?"

"They remind you of various unwanted things."

"So?"

"After a stage they will even start haunting you."

"In any case, I won't throw it away," Ragini insisted.

"You know, why those Telugu people gave up the photo here?"

"I don't know."

"So that they can keep themselves away from such memories of festival seasons."

"I cannot be that much cruel. Anyway, isn't it for keeping the memories of those who have gone before us that we preserve their photos?"

"But these are all memories thrown away by somebody. Only those who can throw away old photographs and seek the nails for new ones at every turning point in life can be called clever. It is for such people that new cities arise."

"In such instances, I would rather go for the old city itself."

When Ragini said this a little adamantly, Viswanathan could not but laugh.

When his son's CD-ROM began to roar violently, his laughter merged into that roar. Thinking about something they returned slowly to the sitting room.

Airships of various shapes are seen on the glittering screen, flying rapidly. A number of robots are sliding down from these ships. They send missiles to the Dark Continent. When the cannons arranged around the fort begin to spit fire the airships disappear.

Their son was jumping up and down, and clapping in great thrill. Viswanathan put his fingers in his ears and Ragini covered her ears with the tip of her sari. On seeing this, the son doubled the volume.

"O God, it's news time again!" Ragini looked at the clock and exclaimed. "Who knows what has happened to that poor Sujatha's daughter?"

When she switched on the TV her son stamped his foot in anger and turned the volume of the computer down.

The news had already started. A lean man with sleepy eyes was reading the news in place of Sujatha. Yawning frequently, he was talking about Croatia. Ragini tried several times to draw his attention, moving her hands and waving her towel. But he didn't seem to notice it. Between yawning and Croatia the annoyance at the loss of sleep was found surging up on his dried face.

When she ran out of patience, Ragini asked loudly:

"Helloooo, is Sujatha there?"

The newsreader did not seem to like that interruption. He raised his face for a moment and turned it down again onto the papers before him. His yawns were now dragged along from Croatia to Bosnia. While talking about Bosnia his displeasure seemed to have doubled.

Knocking on the frame of the TV gently she asked again. She was aware that her voice had risen too much.

"Hey, Mister! Isn't Sujatha on duty now?"

He raised his face again slowly, with displeasure in his drowsy eyes. After a few seconds he said:

"It would be nice if the esteemed viewer lowers her voice."

"I ask you, where is Sujatha?"

"Who knows?"

"She had told me that this news-reading had also been assigned to her."

"But the esteemed viewer can very well see that it is being done by another person."

The increasing displeasure, and the irritation he felt because of his yawn getting broken halfway made him writhe. His eyes reddened. In an attempt to make his eyes clear he shook his head. Then he got confused with the lines of the report and tripped unknowingly from Bosnia onto Kampuchea. Lying there he began to grope for the word that parted from him. On seeing that, Viswanathan winked at Ragini as if telling her that they would get no more news from him henceforth.

"Poor Sujatha! Who knows what has become of her?" while turning the TV off, her eyes were filled with tears.

At the very next moment her son leapt across the room and doubled the volume of the speaker.

Fierce attacks and counter-attacks are seen now on the computer screen. Fire-pits are formed at the places where missiles fall. Columns of smoke rise high. Wave after wave of airships sweep across the sky.

The earth splits and many things are seen sinking to its bottom. When some creatures try to hide underneath the earth, the missiles go down into the abyss so as to pursue them.

On seeing all these, the son goes on clapping and shouting boisterously.

Suddenly a loud noise was heard below.

Viswanathan ran to the balcony, followed by Ragini.

There was a clamour at the other end of the street. All the street lights had gone out.

"I think it is a bomb explosion," Viswanathan said in a frightened tone.

"In our new city too?" Ragini could not believe it.

"Bombs know no boundaries, that too in a complicated city like ours," Viswanathan said; in a calm voice this time. However, Ragini did not discern that calmness.

By then their son had come to the balcony dancing with joy.

"What's the noise down there, dad?"

"Possibly an explosion." Viswanathan hesitated for a moment.

"At last, a bomb in our street too!"

That proximity thrilled him greatly. Roaring with laughter he peered out holding onto the railing of the balcony.

"Are the airships rushing in through the sky? When will the robots slide down? When will be the first lightning attack?" He was greatly excited.

When he asked questions incessantly, Viswanathan could not answer them; nor could Ragini.

"It could be at any time, son," she said vaguely.

Translation of Raṇṭu nagaraṅṅaḷ

+ + +

9

The Hanging of Kumaran

By early morning many people had gathered around the stage set for the hanging of Kumaran. The stage was built beyond the sandy courtyard in the jail compound. There was a black wire fence around it. At the very centre stood the gallows painted pitch black. The trench below the gallows was bridged with a wooden plank. There was a pedestal on the plank, right below the loop of rope that hung from the gallows.

There were four or five rows of cane chairs beyond the fence. Seated on these chairs, the invited audience was waiting impatiently to see the rare spectacle. It is quite some time that a hanging has taken place in the village jail. The two brass-laden thrones draped in red silk covers and placed in the middle of the front row of chairs remained empty though.

Kumaran's wife was sitting at one side of the front row. The four-year-old girl who sat close to her, pressing the belly of a white doll, was Kumaran's daughter. Kumaran's wife was a lean woman with a dark complexion. She was wearing the white clothes worn by a widow. Her head was covered with the tip of her sari. A few curls of hair fell onto her forehead. Her eyes were purple and there was a blank expression on her face.

Seated on the left side of the front row, five or six journalists were engaged in subdued conversation. There was a camera on the lap of the bearded man among them.

"Isn't eight o'clock, the appointed time?" a fat bald-headed journalist with a sunburnt face asked the man sitting beside him.

"I think so."

"But the *Adhikari* and the Commissioner haven't turned up so far."

"They will come. Both of them are very punctual."

At half past seven the Adhikari, the officer-in-charge of the village arrived with a group of people in khaki uniform and red sash. He was tall and lean with the face of a pigeon and a prominent Adam's apple. Opening the gate of the fence, the Adhikari and his men entered the fenced area and moved onto the stage. After examining certain measurements of the stage with his feet, the officer glanced around the stage. Then he mounted the pedestal, holding on to the gallows and stamped on it thrice in order to ensure that it was sufficiently strong. When he stood up straight, he found that the loop was much above his head. He could just touch it by stretching out his hand.

"How tall is Kumaran?" he asked, looking down.

"Five foot nine," one of the men in khaki uniform said.

"The measurement should be correct. There shouldn't be any raising or lowering of the loop at the time of the hanging. Everything should be perfect. Don't you know the Commissioner's nature?"

The man in uniform nodded. Adhikari climbed down from the pedestal. Then he walked round the gallows and pushed the plank gently to see that it turned properly.

"Once the rope is put round his neck and the lever is pushed, he should remain hanging until he dies. You can loosen the rope afterwards, so that the body will fall into the trench below straight away. I am happy that everything has been arranged well. Though I have supervised several hangings, I am always doubtful whether the final arrangements are foolproof. Everything should be done with meticulous care. Besides, the Commissioner is very strict about these small things. You know his temperament. If he is in a foul mood, whatever good we do will go against us."

Although the Adhikari was visibly nervous he tried to put on a brave face and waved at the audience with a broad smile. Then he walked out of the fenced area. While closing the wire gate again he asked the uniformed man who was following him close behind like his shadow:

"Is Suleiman ready?"

"Yes. At 7.45 Suleiman and Kuppuchamy will bring Kumaran."

Adhikari made a throaty sound meaning 'OK'. Then he repeated what he said earlier:

"Everything should be perfect and there shouldn't be even a minor deviation from the instructions from above. When the Commissioner arrives at 7.55, he should see that everything is ok. Don't you know his nature? If there is any lapse anywhere, I may be the man hanged in place of Kumaran...."

Walking towards the audience the Adhikari settled down in one of the empty chairs among the journalists. "Though it is early in the morning it is quite hot already," he said, fanning himself with a bunch of papers.

"Yes, yes," the journalist with the gold-rimmed spectacles, sitting next to him smiled. "It is almost impossible to go outdoors by eight or nine o'clock; we start sweating heavily."

The Adhikari kept silent for some time. He was thinking about something. After a while he asked:

"Haven't you all got the press brief?"

"Yeah," the journalists said.

"Good. If you have any doubts, you can ask me now. I have come here to give a proper briefing to the media and the people alike. The Commissioner is very particular about the media coverage. I needn't tell you about his nature."

The journalist with the gold-rimmed spectacles nodded his head with a beam. His golden teeth and spectacles shone brightly in the morning sunlight.

"You have mentioned everything with minute details in the write-up; about Kumaran, his past record, family background, the final judgement and so on. We had already covered almost all these things, many times in the past; haven't we, Chellappan master?" He looked at his elder colleague.

"The brochure, however, doesn't say about the crimes committed by Kumaran," said Chellappan master, "and about the arguments of the defence."

"What arguments, what defence?" The Adhikari chuckled "It's a fool proof case, where no trial is required. Still the authorities were fair enough to give him an opportunity to give his version...."

"Then?" Chellappan Master was visibly surprised, "We haven't heard about it. Or for that matter anyone in the media. Even the governmental media...."

The man with gold-rimmed spectacles nodded in agreement.

The Adhikari pretended not to have heard it and closed his eyes, brooding on something else.

"This is my twenty fifth stage," he said suddenly.

"Really, great! That means this is a silver jubilee function! We didn't have even the faintest idea about it. Anyway, let us publish a special box item on this rare achievement; shall we, Chellappan master?"

Chellappan master nodded reluctantly. When the bubbles of sweat sprouted between his greying crew cut hair, he began to scratch his head with his long nails. Then the mixed smell of sweat, rancid oil and dandruff spread in the air.

"When was the first scene of hanging enacted under your direction? Who was the actor?" the man with gold-rimmed spectacles asked with a wry smile on his face.

"It was a nineteen-year-old boy," the Adhikari said, going back into his memories.

"What was the crime he committed?"

"Crime...? I don't remember it. It was five or six years ago. Anyway, it is none of our concern. We have a job to do and we are quite clear about it. However, I remember one thing. The boy's eyebrows were thick and broad. While his body was hanging on the gallows with his teeth clenched, the curved eyebrows resembled a black bow. To tell you the truth, I couldn't sleep on the following two or three nights. Whenever I shut my eyes, his eyebrows came to my mind...."

"That was because it was your first experience. Now you have become an expert." The man with the gold-rimmed spectacles laughed.

The Adhikari was filled with pride and began to fumble with the buttons of his shirt.

After a while the sound of a bugle was heard.

Below the granite arch of the jail the iron gate opened with a groan. The black, lean figure of Kumaran appeared with two executioners in black dress on either side. The gate was closed again with a groan. They walked slowly towards the stage. Kumaran's hands were tied behind. While walking between the two gigantic figures, his bent body swayed a little. His beard had grown by a few months, and hair fell over his shoulders. He had changed from the jail clothes into casual clothes, a long brown coarse Kurta and a dirty dhoti. He was barefooted.

Kumaran's face was calm.

The Adhikari rose to his feet and hurried towards them. He received them just outside the wire fence and smiled at Suleiman and Kuppuchamy.

"Is everything ready?" he asked them.

"Yeah," Suleiman grunted like a wild buffalo. His face was cruel. A pair of black eyes burned below his unibrow. His droopy moustache twitched. When he parted his red, thick lips slightly, his dirty, red teeth emitted the smell of blood.

The Adhikari squeezed Kumaran's hands and said gently:

"Please don't hate me." His voice quivered suddenly. The bulge on his throat rose and fell. "This is my duty; just as dying is Kumaran's duty."

Kumaran did not say anything. Not even a single muscle of his calm face moved. He stood staring into the distance, waiting to take the next step. "I was just saying," the Adhikari continued. "How can I live in this world with your curse on me?"

"It's time, Let us go," Suleiman grunted.

"Yes, it's time," the Adhikari said with a start, looking at his watch. "It's time for the Commissioner to arrive; hurry up!"

When they came near the pedestal, the Adhikari told Kumaran: "Pay obeisance to the pedestal, because you are going on a long journey...."

Kumaran did not listen to his words. He climbed onto the pedestal slowly. While putting the loop round Kumaran's neck, Suleiman chanted: "In the name of God, the most merciful...."

The audience clapped.

The bald-headed man looked at Kumaran's wife. Her face had become tight. She was staring at the loop without batting an eyelid; whereas, her daughter was still fumbling with the doll. Doesn't this woman feel like crying at least! The bald-headed man wondered. Why has she come to witness this terrible scene? Didn't Kumaran die in her mind on the day the judge passed the sentence? He found sleepless nights dozing in her black, swollen eyes. He tried to follow the memories passing through her mind. It might be the memories of an event that took place years ago on a similar stage. She was sitting in the middle of an audience. Similar to what has happened to her husband just now, a loop of sweet smelling flowers was put round her neck also. It was a loop of love and a lifelong bondage. In front of the holy fire, with the priest chanting various mantras, she felt the gentle touch of a warm palm causing her blood to flow suddenly from finger tips to head.

The bugle sounded again. The audience twisted their heads suddenly in the direction from where the sound was heard. A few men in khaki uniform with red sash were marching to the compound. Behind them was the Commissioner in black suit. His young wife was also with him, walking on his left side. She was wearing a black sari.

The Adhikari ran forward and received them with a salute. Suleiman and Kuppuchamy, who were standing erect on either side of the gallows, also saluted the Commissioner. The audience rose to their feet and bowed. After returning the salutes, and bowing to the audience the Commissioner sat on the throne.

"Is everything ready?" the Commissioner asked, turning his head towards the Adhikari.

"Yes, sir."

"Isn't it scheduled for eight o'clock?"

"Yes, sir."

"Perhaps it will have to be delayed a little; five or six minutes. Some guests are coming."

"OK, sir."

The Commissioner looked around and smiled at the journalists.

"Has the Adhikari briefed you well?" he asked the journalists.

"Yes, sir," the man with the gold-rimmed spectacles said. "He has done everything meticulously. Even otherwise, we will report it properly."

"I know it," the Commissioner said with satisfaction. "Your write-ups can influence the people greatly. We are only officials, bound to obey the orders of the authorities up above. We don't have any sway similar to the one you people have over the public. Even the khaki uniform is abominable to the people...."

"No, sir. It is not so now. What you said was true in the past. Public attitude has changed, however, ever since you have taken charge."

The Commissioner was immensely pleased and looked at his wife with a smile as if asking 'haven't you heard what he said?' She did not see it, however. Her eyes were fixed on the black skinny figure standing in the middle of the stage. She scanned that figure several times, and after each scanning her eyes returned to the loop over his head. The sight of the loop disturbed her very much. When she was in college, the Crucifixion was enacted there. Rajan played the role of Jesus. He was a man with sparkling eyes, sunken cheeks and a thin beard. His calm eyes and resounding voice had a mesmerising power. So many girls in the college had become slaves to his eyes and voice. Here is another crucifixion on a different stage. This man has a resemblance to Rajan. The same eyes and beard.... Can his voice also be the same?

When the Commissioner pinched her thigh unobserved by others, she jolted out of her thoughts and looked around in bewilderment.

"There's a disturbed look on your face; what's wrong?" the Commissioner asked her kindly.

"Oh, nothing."

"You look pale, anyway."

"It just seems to you so."

"See, a Commissioner's wife should never be sentimental. You will have to appear as a distinguished guest before several stages like this.

"Stage...!" she muttered. "Whenever I am a viewer, only crucifixion is enacted on the stage. The same Jesus is crucified repeatedly in different forms. The same Jews come in different attires to crucify him."

"Today is our wedding anniversary," the Commissioner reminded her, sitting closer to her. "This is the grandest stage you can expect on a special occasion like this."

She kept silent. Her eyes once again strayed over to the gallows and the loop. He, Rajan, was still standing in the same posture. His hands and legs were not moving at all. He did not even bat an eyelid. On seeing the blank expression on his face several questions came to her mind.

Has his mind also become blank? What is he thinking? Does he repent now? Or is he praying?

The sun had risen to the top of the granite wall like a red-hot metal disc. The stage was covered in the blazing sunlight. Suleiman was visibly angry as he was forced to wait near the gallows, soaked in sweat. He was scratching his body with his hands under the thick black dress, unobserved by others. He had not eaten anything since daybreak, as has been his practice all along. He will have his belly full after the function and a cold shower.

An attendant brought an umbrella and held it over the heads of the Commissioner and his wife.

The bald-headed man looked at his watch. It's 8.15. Why is it getting delayed further? Who are these so important guests?

Kumaran's wife was still sitting in the same posture; staring into the hollow space with the same blank expression on her face. Moving onto the chair next to her, the bald-headed man asked her in a low voice:

"Don't you feel sad, sister?"

She turned her face and looked at him. Their eyes met, but she made no reply. She might be wondering why there was an unusual kindness in his eyes.

"No, I am not sad," she whispered suddenly. "I have never had any desire in my life. Hence I don't feel sad."

"Isn't your husband sad?"

Once the words were out of his mouth, he realised that he shouldn't have asked that cruel and unnecessary question. However, she replied in a calm voice without thinking even for a second:

"No, he is also not likely to be sad. He has been expecting this moment for years; if not in this form, in some other form."

The daughter turned her attention from the doll to the stage all of a sudden. She gazed at the sunlit stage with a perplexed look and asked:

"Who is that man, mother?"

"That's your father. He was sent to prison while you were a little child."

"Why is my father standing there? Is he going to perform circus?"

The mother could not answer her questions.

"This is the Adhikari's silver jubilee hanging," the man with the gold-rimmed spectacles told the Commissioner as if cracking a joke.

"Is it?" the Commissioner expressed surprise. "I didn't know it. The Adhikari hasn't told me so far. Smart man! Congratulations! Let us celebrate it, anyway...."

The Officer laughed politely, putting his hand over his mouth.

"How many years are left for your retirement?"

"Seven years, sir."

"Good. So you have ample time to complete a century. Best of luck!"

"Thank you, sir."

"What did you say?" the Commissioner's wife asked him with a startled expression on her face.

"I was saying that the Adhikari has ample time to hit a century!"

"That means...," she paused for a while and continued: "he has got enough time to string a hundred fingers into a garland and to wear it around his neck, doesn't it?"

The Commissioner simply laughed.

"Come with me, Ramakrishnan," the Adhikari gestured to the press photographer. "Before the guests arrive we can go to the stage and look for the right placement for the camera. As you know this is a split second action and I doubt whether you have that kind of a high-speed camera to capture the moments in its entirety. This silver jubilee write-up should carry some unique photographs also. The sort of thing one hasn't seen earlier."

The photographer nodded in agreement and they walked hurriedly towards the stage. Ramakrishnan looked at the gallows from different angles and examined various angles; standing, sitting and lying sideways. Then he asked for a stool and one of the men in uniform brought it. The photographer stepped onto the stool and looked at the loop, standing on tiptoes. His face brightened. "We can take the photo from here, Sir. Lighting will be all right. If it is taken as light and shade the profile shot will be simply amazing. It will be a marvellous combination of the black gallows with white sky in the background, the neck hanging on the black rope and the artificial shades round the tongue that is sticking out from the mouth. I have never got an opportunity to do this kind of a work. Ramakrishnan's imagination was roused. It spread its wings and began to fly. He jumped down from the stool. Hugging the camera he jumped up and down.

"But one thing," Ramakrishnan reminded the Adhikari. "After the hanging, his head should not bend too much. If it is so, the camera won't be able to pick up his facial expressions. Let him hold his face up as much as possible. Then only we will get a good profile."

The Adhikari came near Kumaran. "Don't be angry with me, Kumaran; don't hate me either." His voice wavered. "This is my duty; just as dying is yours. So, please cooperate with us. Things have come this far, anyway. Hence, do us the favour of holding your head up before the loop is tightened. Don't trouble the photographer. He is an artist."

At that moment Ramakrishnan interrupted:

"You were also an artist, Kumaran! It's only once in a blue moon that we get a rare shot like this. If my picture turns out to be not as expected.... I am sure that Kumaran can understand the agony of an artist...."

"OK, OK. Enough," the Adhikari intervened. "Our Kumaran will oblige. Come, let's get out of here."

While they were walking out, Suleiman called out from behind angrily: "Isn't it time for the hanging?"

"A few minutes more. Two more guests are yet to come."

"I have been melting in the sun for a long time. May I change out of this black dress?"

"No, Suleiman! Don't spoil the beauty of the stage," the Adhikari implored him.

At that moment a jeep came roaring and stopped outside the fence. Five foreigners jumped down from it. They had long copper-coloured hair and beard. The loose shirts they wore were dirty. They were carrying cameras over their shoulders. The Commissioner rose to his feet and waved his hand. They moved towards him. They were journalists from abroad. The Commissioner introduced them to the other journalists. They exchanged smiles and shook hands with each other.

"Sorry, we are late, aren't we? These hotel guys, you know, they delayed the breakfast."

"It's all right. We were waiting for you. You won't get this kind of a scene anywhere in the world," The man with the gold-rimmed spectacles said.

"We know it. That's why we have come all the way not to miss this opportunity. Anyway, we won't cause further delay. Give us just a couple of minutes for setting our cameras."

They ran towards the wire fence and fixed their cameras on the tripods. Then looking through the lenses of the cameras they decided upon the angles from which the photos were to be taken. They had highly sophisticated equipment with them.

"The stage is becoming grander. What an amazing experience!" The Commissioner was thrilled. "We won't get a better treat than this on the special occasion of our wedding anniversary." He put his hand affectionately on his wife's shoulder.

"Eh? What did you say?" She asked with a start. As he kept silent she repeated the question impatiently.

"I didn't say anything," he said in a displeased tone.

"This is a rare scene, ma'am." A blonde girl among the foreign journalists told the Commissioner's wife. "In our country hanging has been abolished. We use the electric chair instead. Joe has some rare pics from the Nazi camps. However, he will never get anything like this elsewhere. Look at the man to be hanged. How photogenic he is!"

"Yes, photogenic, indeed," the Commissioner's wife muttered. Rajan was equally photogenic.

The sun was blazing down from the sky. Light melted and flowed down onto the stage. Unable to bear the scorching heat and the calls from the empty stomach, Suleiman writhed and gnashed his teeth. He was shivering with rage. He yearned to throw away the black dress that was sticking to his body, and to tear apart the sinner standing before him so that everything will come to an end instantly. In his madding rage he desired even to dance on the stage, bathed in blood and wearing the other man's intestines round his neck as a garland. 'I am the Goddess of death' he thought.

When everything was ready the Commissioner rose to his feet and held his black gloved hand extended towards the stage. Standing face to face with the Commissioner, the Adhikari saluted him. Then he turned round and shouted:

"Everybody ready! Set the cameras."

"Roger," the foreigners said.

"Ramakrishnan..."

"Ready, sir..."

"Suleiman..."

Suleiman snorted.

"Kumaran... action..."

There was no reply from Kumaran; not even a stir.

"Okay, then. Everybody ready..."

"Start..." the Adhikari roared.

Sitting on the throne to the left of the Commissioner, Kumaran watched the scene calmly. The Commissioner's wife was standing in black dress on the red pedestal. Suleiman put the loop round her neck. Kuppuchamy gave a push to the plank and the pedestal turned upside down. The neck hanging in the loop resembled the white, fragile neck of a bird. Her body convulsed just once; face swelled up; tongue stuck out; eyes remained half-closed; and head bent down to her chest. By then the rope was loosened and that white female body in black dress fell into the trench with a thud.

Translation of Araṅṅ

✦ ✦ ✦

10

On the Stage

It was after fixing the appointment over the telephone that Sarada came to meet me. When she entered the room I noticed the tension on her face. Casting a bewildered look on all sides she closed the door. Her face had become tight. The journey in the burning sun had reddened it as well.

"The door needn't be shut," I said with a smile.

"Let it remain closed, sir; for the things I want to tell you..."

"You can tell me anything, no problem. In my case, however, there are only very few secrets."

She did not say anything for some time. Her eyes were moving along the paintings on the wall. An unusual grey tinge was seen on her face. Her eyes seemed very small because of being tearful. The lower eyelids were a little swollen and tinged with dark shades.

"During the last three or four days I was thinking about some unwanted things," she whispered a little dramatically.

An actress with make-up on her face is standing in the middle of the stage. When she gets a chance she goes near the mike, walking with slow steps befitting the seriousness of the situation, and makes an important announcement to the audience. The modulation of her voice is something deliberate. Concealing her internal turmoil strenuously, she manages to utter it in an emotionless, clear and resounding voice with a view to shocking and disturbing the audience. This direct announcement to the audience is just the beginning of a number of outbursts that are yet to occur on the stage.

Sarada was still looking at my face. She seemed to doubt whether I had heard her words properly and taken them in all seriousness.

I asked her to be seated. She wiped her face with the ends of her sari and sat on the sofa. I was watching her swollen eyes and puffed up face. She seemed like the typical unhappy girl from the soap operas.

"During the last three or four days I was pondering about something drastic, sir."

"I heard you mention it earlier."

"But you haven't understood what I meant." I could read these words from her displeased face.

"Suicide, perhaps," she said vaguely and glanced at me.

I smiled.

"You see, nobody should make such casual statements about suicide.' I said. "Those who decide to commit suicide will not go around telling others. They do it instead and in a way that they find suitable. Casual statements about such things doesn't have any relevance or news value; especially in the present day when the number of people committing suicide has increased substantially."

She didn't seem to like what I said. Her face reddened further. Her hand shivered when she wiped her face and neck with her sari.

"I know you are on Satheesh's side. Men are always like that. They remain united in such matters."

After saying this she moved slowly towards the window. Raising her right hand she opened one of the window panes slowly and began to look at the vehicles plying along the road below. A shaft of sunlight was falling on her face.

"Stupid!" I muttered.

Nothing goes wrong with the laid down norms. Each step is timed perfectly. A great deal of practice has gone into it. Moving towards the window, raising the right hand slowly and opening the window pane in a leisurely manner and then looking down onto the road tilting the head a little...

This scene is closer to a movie than to a drama – a side-pose on the spot marked by the cameraman. Only half of the face on which light falls, can be seen clearly. The other parts, namely the long hair, blue blouse and the sari with blue spots can all be seen vaguely in the faint light inside the room.

"Men are always so," she repeated. "All men think and behave in the same manner; even you, sir."

I simply laughed. As you know, I was the only viewer of the scenes enacted on that stage.

Sarada does not turn her face. Her eyes are still on the road. It cannot be left unsaid that her posture is quite graceful. The hum of the camera can be heard clearly. She will turn her face only when the director shouts 'action'.

It will always be a sudden dramatic twist of the face along with an agitated dialogue. Only such lines that can move the viewers will be in the script. After filming the scene, the camera will zoom in for a tight close-up. The twisting of the face in close-up and repetition of the piercing dialogue! There again is the possibility of filming the same scene in two angles; the rest will be done by the editor.

"Don't you support Satheesh always?" she asked without turning her face.

In the normal case, whether it is a drama or a movie, I should rise to my feet slowly at this juncture and move towards her; something called a mid-shot.

But I didn't try to do so. Remaining seated on the sofa and lighting up a cigarette I said casually:

"Where is the question of support here? Why should I take an interest in your family matters?"

It was just a lifeless statement. Still I felt a little amused when I made it, and wondered whether I could ease the tension caused by the emotionalism displayed on the stage till then.

Whether it is on the stage or in the tennis court, both the players should go ahead with the same speed, rhythm, and determination. Otherwise, the whole show will be spoilt. If one is indifferent, the other will be confused. There is a tempo for everything. Once it is lost, a lot of time will be required to build it up again.

However, my words do not seem to have made any impact on Sarada. She continues in the same posture. The camera is groaning. The director may have fallen asleep, leaving nobody to say 'cut'.

I felt it improper to let it go on endlessly. Hence I asked:

"What is the new issue? Have you become estranged from Satheesh again?

These questions elicited some response from her. She turned her head round suddenly and flung a few words back at me:

"Your question is quite irrelevant, since we have never been in harmony. Sir, you can't imagine the miseries my son and I have suffered during the last four years...," just the same words.

Moving four or five steps away from the window she had come close to my sofa now and was talking loudly to me looking at my face and raising her hand. However, I didn't listen to her words, for the things she said had nothing to do with me. The actress who was performing well before me was not related to me; she was only my colleague. Six or seven years ago she happened to fall in love with somebody in the office; the usual thing in an office. Her lover was one Satheesh. He was also something like an actor; neither a hero nor a villain. When their affair became serious, it created a lot of problems. Since they belonged to different castes, their families as well as the people in their localities opposed it strongly. Naturally there followed a torrent of allegations, threats and anonymous letters....

Sarada continues her spectacular performance before a totally disinterested viewer.

'Therefore, therefore...," she shouts. Her hair is falling loosely over her shoulder. The saffron mark on her forehead is drenched in sweat. All the tensions that a heroine usually experiences when the drama is nearing the climax can be seen on Sarada's face. She is spitting out all the dialogues that she has learned and the ones that came to her mind. Excellent modulation of sound, clear delivery and perfect timing! She does not need the mike at all. She is capable of entertaining an audience in a temple compound, without allowing them to boo even if the lights go off during the performance.

"Stop it," I said loudly, raising my hand. "Who are you to me?"

She did not say anything. She was panting because of the exertion she made hitherto, and was trying to ease her breathing. The limitations of the script worried her and she groped for the unwritten lines.

"Who is your Satheesh to me?" I asked again. She made no reply to this question as well.

"Now I realise that it was foolish on my part to function as a mediator between you and take great pains to unite you in marriage."

Just the usual words again, but I hoped that on realising the hollowness and powerlessness of my words she would decide not to continue her performance before a man like me.

However, nothing of the kind occurred. There was no change of expression on her face. She continued to be relentless and became more excited.

"You became a mediator voluntarily. We hadn't requested you to take up that role."

Here the old story reaches an important turning point.

The affair between Sarada and Satheesh had come to a standstill. Their colleagues, who used to whisper to each other and smile meaningfully looking at the lovers, ceased to notice them. The gossips spread about them seemed to have been forgotten by everybody. Now all of a sudden they appear to have become just an ordinary man and woman; two persons working in the same office, sitting next to each other. They come to the office in time, do their work, crack harmless jokes occasionally, eat together, exchange the food materials and so on; just an ordinary situation. It appeared that they forgot everything related to their love when it became stale and the devil went out of their heads. Or did they become fed up with it? Anyway, they could become good colleagues just as they were in the past.

However, I, the superintendent of the office could not understand this sudden change in their relationship. How can one believe that such a strong love that existed between them can be so short-lived? Wasn't there anything between them other than the mere attraction between a man and a woman who used to sit in adjacent chairs for five or six years? If their love was not something closely knit, and they didn't have the feeling that either of them would cease to exist in the absence of the other, why did they ponder about troublesome things like elopement and getting married at a Registrar's office?

I found it extremely boring. What I had learned about man-woman relationship seemed to turn upside down. I realised that their love had not taken roots in their minds as an intense emotional turmoil. When I shared my thoughts with my wife she laughed: "Don't intervene in it. This is how inter-caste relationships end up always. When the initial zest dies down, the lovers will begin to quarrel over silly things. Don't you know the case of my classmate Indira? Anyway, Sarada and Satheesh are lucky that they haven't got married."

However, I could not agree with what my wife said. While they were in intense love, I could see a peculiar glitter in their eyes. Can such things cease all of a sudden? How much excited they might have been when they loved each other passionately?

"What are you thinking, sir?" Sarada asked me.

She had cooled down a little. She was sitting curled up on the sofa, and I had no idea what was in her mind at that time.

In a sense what Sarada said was true. I had a role in warming up their love that had become cold; but what was wrong with it? After getting involved in a burning love affair for a long period the lovers begin to behave as mere colleagues all of a sudden! I could not digest it. When I talked about it to Thomas he evaded the issue with a smile and warned me: "Don't intervene in it, sir. It's a disgraceful affair. Let them do whatever they like." What Karthikeyan did, however, was to give the dirty colour of an office gossip to their relationship and laughed a lot.

Anyway, I could not conform to their stand. It was not just an issue of inter-caste marriage. Some basic concepts about the man-woman relationship were getting disproved here. I found some sort of incongruity in the demise of their love. Some fundamental issues concerning the integrity of the society were also involved in it. I thought it would be wrong to ignore it. The precedence they were creating would mislead even future generations.

However, at that juncture of complete standstill things took a dramatic turn all of a sudden.

I think it was the unexpected words from my mouth that roused Sarada and revived her love for Satheesh. I don't remember what I said exactly. It was something like this: "Love has a spiritual dimension. Instead of treating it as a mere fancy, it should be considered as an everlasting relationship rooted in the soul. Those who are not pure at heart should not get involved in a love affair."

What I said must have hit somewhere in her mind and lingered there. Anyway, things moved very fast thereafter. In spite of the strong objections from their families, they eloped one day, after midnight and went into hiding for some days. And finally, when they went to the Registrar's office I was with them in the taxi and signed in the register as one of the witnesses.

"When we found ourselves quarrelling repeatedly before the marriage itself, we realised that we wouldn't be a good match for each other. Hence we put an end to our romance; but you intervened at this juncture and persuaded us to revive our relationship."

Sarada is wiping her eyes. After the spectacular performance on the stage the heroine is very tired now. For a long time hence she is only able to sob, whimper and wipe her eyes. The instrumentalists sitting behind the curtain have a busy time now.

"Now you put all the blame on me, Sarada? Anyway, I realise that a mediator's role is highly boring; especially in the case of marriages."

"I didn't say so. Still, there is no denying the fact that if you hadn't roused us we would have gone two ways."

"Okay, what was it that I told you then?"

"I don't remember it exactly. You said something regarding purity. That means you were hinting that our behaviour hitherto was quite cheap and devoid of purity. By God! We hadn't spoilt our purity. So your remark made us determined to get married at any cost."

I sat stunned for a while. They had jumped into a troublesome marriage without understanding the least what I actually meant! What a misunderstanding!

"Anyway, do you think what you did was wrong, Sarada?"

She did not reply. After sitting with her head drooped for a while, she raised her head slowly and looked at me intensely. Tears welled up in her eyes again. She tried to say something and swallowed the words immediately. Though she said nothing, I could read her mind to some extent. She would not admit that her decision was wrong. Several memorable things might be there piled up in her mind. There are so many women living in the memories of the past, by rewinding the frames of such rare moments.

"Do you hate your husband now?"

"Husband!" Sarada snorted and jumped to her feet.

The scene changes suddenly. The heroine's face becomes tight and flushed. There is a haunted look in her eyes. It seems yet another move to the climax.

What she said must be true. One will not become a husband by simply signing in the thick book kept in the Registrar's office, without observing the customary rituals associated with a marriage.

"Don't get upset, Sarada. Tell me what has happened. What is the problem between you and Satheesh? Let us try to solve it."

"I don't want any kind of solution. Nobody should try for that."

"Then what are you going to do?"

"I want a divorce."

"You talked about suicide a little while ago?"

"That is another option."

"Which would happen first?—The divorce or the suicide?"

"This is not the time for jokes. I have come here for some serious talk."

It is here that we get confused in understanding the female characters. Things would have become highly complicated if I had made arrangements for her suicide, with the same interest that I took in the case of her marriage. Female characters require a lot of time for rethinking. Sarada had not thought seriously about committing suicide, considering it as something inevitable. She was casually talking about it, without showing the least emotional disturbance caused by such a drastic move. In case she did commit suicide, she would find it a folly on rethinking later on. Then wouldn't her soul start hunting me as the man responsible for her death, just as she disowned the responsibility of her marriage and made me the culprit in it?

"Then what about divorce?"

"No, there is no change in that decision," she said firmly.

"Will you say later on that it could have been avoided?"

"Never."

"Has Satheesh consented to it?"

"Who wants his consent?"

"If either of you is against divorce, it will become a court case; and there will arise the question of your son's future."

"I will tell the court that I don't want even a farthing from that guy."

"If you have already taken the decision, why have you come here?"

She fumbled for words, for she seemed to have forgotten why she had come all the way to meet me.

I wondered whether she had hoped to revive the lost intimacy between her and Satheesh, hanging on to some unexpected statement that might slip from my mouth. Since it was I who had patched up their broken relationship once, she had every right to hope so.

The possibility for such reconciliation, however, seems very bleak. Her performance on the stage in front of me today proves it. What an amazing performance! She has gained a lot of guts during the last five of six years. This artist is getting better and better with the passage of time.

"There will be a dispute regarding the custody of the child."

"I won't give my son to him at any cost."

"Things are not so easy. A father also has a claim on the child in the eyes of the court."

"If he doesn't give my son to me I will kill him; I don't fear going to the jail."

This also was a vague statement. I began to feel bored. It was a holiday. I had to go out to see a friend. I didn't like wasting a precious day watching her performance, which was lacking in concentration. Hence I interrupted her:

"Look Sarada, any drama requires a powerful script. Each character has a specific function to perform. It is true that talented actors make some slight deviations from the script according to their power of imagination. Such deviations, however, should be in tune with the overall purpose of the drama. If there is no focus in the performance of the actors, the audience will boo. Sometimes they may pelt rotten eggs or even stones. That is what happens here. You continue to say several things without the least compactness before a helpless viewer. Though you are just an amateur actress, you should not display this much vacillation on the stage. Don't forget your duty to the audience. That is the first lesson in the science of histrionics."

Sarada did not like what I said.

"Do you think I have come here to enact a drama? If so, you have made a wrong estimation about me, sir. Both of us come from reputed families."

I changed my approach.

"Look Sarada, the ways before you are very clear. One of them is that of a decent divorce. If that is not acceptable to you, either you kill Satheesh or kill yourself. You can do any of the three on your own without much difficulty. There is no need for a third person or a consultant here. Besides, you have the backing of our great literature and cinema. However, let me tell you one thing. Keep your mind clean while doing anything. Think deeply in solitude about what you are going to do; with the purity akin to meditation. Then do it systematically without any confusion."

"You are talking vaguely again, sir. You don't realise how anguished I am. It was with such a talk about purity that you prompted us to get married."

"Then what should I say?"

"Have you ever tried to find out where Satheesh and I went wrong?"

"I didn't think it necessary."

"That's the problem. Now I realise the folly of doing anything as advised by somebody who is not related to me. Sir, it is common knowledge that marriage is a very important event in one's life. In our younger days we cherished several dreams regarding it. We recollect our wedding ceremony not as some still photographs in an album, but as long scenes; glamorous and colourful scenes. At least for one day in our life other people treat us like king and queen; isn't it true, sir?"

"Yeah, possibly," I muttered, without showing much interest.

"Was my marriage anything of that kind? Haven't we gone wrong right from the beginning? A midnight elopement in an old taxi, just as what we see in some movies! Spending some days in hiding in a friend's house and its tension! And finally, signing in a torn book kept on a dusty table in front of a graceless officer in a leaking office! Is a wedding ceremony complete with these adventures and formalities alone? In the officer's eyes our lives were similar to two moth-eaten title deeds. To get married in a dirty office where buying and selling is the only business done! That was the mistake. If the beginning itself is not in a proper way, everything will be in disorder."

"What are you driving at?"

"If he had tied the *mangalsutra* in my neck in front of Lord Guruvayoorappan in the presence of our kith and kin, he wouldn't have behaved so irresponsibly towards me. At the time of my marriage I didn't have the faintest knowledge that anything done against the customs would turn out to be a disaster like this. Those who should have told me about it didn't do so."

I was absolutely astounded. Yet another accusation!

The drama has reached a new turning point now. She is entering the troublesome areas like tradition and custom. Even though she has mentioned them vaguely, these are all big things. They cannot be presented through some lifeless words uttered on the stage. They have the backing and sturdiness of the faith of generations.

"In a sense it is true," Sarada said as if to herself. "Though we belong to dignified families we broke away from the tradition, and that was the greatest mistake on our part."

"So...?"

Sarada kept silent. She was thinking. Her eyes fell on something at a distance, out of the window. Her ancestors must have been marching through her mind with vigour and vindictiveness. A female descendant at the long end of the chain, who took a wrong step and slipped down, is now eyeing to walk through their footsteps. The upswell of emotions within her was getting reflected on her face. Tears welled up in her eyes. She said in a hoarse, wavered and subdued voice:

"So... so..., if possible, one more wedding ceremony in a traditional manner before Lord Guruvayoorappan. Let my son be a witness to it. As it is held now, the families of both of us will attend the function. People may laugh at us, but I don't care. Let it be a new beginning. If this one also fails...."

I was sitting stunned. A fourth option appearing from nowhere!

"Things have come this far, anyway. Do me this favour alone. People may ridicule us; it doesn't matter. Please do this for me."

I did not reply, because I didn't have anything to say. My fingers were desperately groping for the string to draw the curtain down.

Translation of Araṅṅatt

✦ ✦ ✦

11

The Gramophone

Long, long ago there was a music box in our house—a very old gramophone. My mother's eldest brother, Raman uncle had brought it from Rangoon. We, the children liked its long, spittoon-like speaker and the picture of the dog listening to his master's voice. It was with great admiration that we watched Raman uncle wind it up occasionally by turning its handle, and changing the small needles at the tip of its arm with great care.

There were a number of lined discs kept in beautiful covers with the colourful photos of film stars printed on them. We were amazed to learn that those lines on these discs were full of songs. Through those mournful songs, K.L. Saigal, Pankaj Mallik and C.H Atma entered our house and became regulars thereafter. Their resonant voices filled our dark and windy monsoon nights with melancholy. We, the children also felt sad when we watched the glum flame of the kerosene lamp flicker when these voices floated in the air.

'Why this uncle does not play any songs that are pleasant to the ears?'

This question was written on our faces and also in the eyes of our dog, Kitchu. Whenever uncle began to play the gramophone, Kitchu's head appeared outside the window. Pressing his face against the bars of the window he would stare at the speaker of the gramophone. We were not sure whether he was interested in the song or the picture of his playmate on the revolving disc.

The photo of Raman uncle, wearing an ash-coloured coat and a stylish felt hat had been hanging on the wall in the southern room for ages. He almost looked like an English man minus their pompous pipe. Since the room always remained locked we used to peep into it through the window with great admiration. At last, we also have a white man in our family, the first man to go abroad from the village during the war time, that too in a huge ship. Hence we were a bit disappointed to see his real figure when he returned home from Rangoon unannounced one evening. A porter, a boy in khaki shorts, was carrying his trunks and a couple of jute bags. Even our mother could not recognise him at first; because it was not the same handsome young man who had left the shores a couple of decades back. An odd looking old man with a grey beard, crumpled coat and shabby trousers.

On entering the verandah, he called out in a tired voice.

"Ammootty, I am back..."

My mother, who appeared from nowhere, was shaken by the strange frail figure at the doorstep. She looked at him in bewilderment.

"I am back at last, Ammootty." He repeated. "And may not return also." There was a sense of relief in his voice.

"Why?"

"I am fed up, Ammootty!"

"Have you come alone?"

"Yeah."

"What about your family?"

"I just came, that's all."

These were the only clear words that we ever heard from Raman uncle; since we did not hear his voice thereafter.

The porter was waiting for his wages and seeing the helplessness on uncle's face, Amma paid the boy off.

We watched Amma clean up the southern room quietly with a broom stick and the servant maid Janu was also summoned hurriedly from the neighbouring house to clean the floor with wet cloth and also to change the old linens on the bed.

Meanwhile, Raman uncle stood at the door step in silent amusement and slowly entered the room watchfully when it was declared fit enough for his stay.

That was perhaps the last occasion on which we children could have a full glimpse of the great man we all had adored right from our early days. In fact, he was the pride of the family, if not of the village as such, since the old timers used to talk eloquently about his brilliance, and how the British professors at the Maharaja's college, Ernakulam adored his command of English and the ability to give extempore speeches on Shakespeare's tragedies.

But that room remained closed thereafter....

Whenever I peeped into the room through the windows that was left ajar, I saw him stretched out on the armchair reading a thickly bound book. When he looked at us with a pale smile through his thick glasses with thin silver frames, we felt something odd. This is not the same old Raman uncle on the wall, we are familiar with.

We noticed that the songs of Saigal, Mallik and Athma were flowing out of that room at all times.

"Ramettan is all sorrows," Amma told us one day.

We also chanted in unison among ourselves.

"Raman uncle is all sorrows."

We were told that he used to come out of the room at noon for lunch, that too after a few impatient knocks at the door by Amma. But we missed those rare occasions, since we were in the school at that time. Of course, his supper was only a small plantain and a glass of milk.

After a few months, he stopped that also. He refused to come out of the room, saying that his eyes would burn on looking at the sunlight; and insisted that the meals should be served in the room itself.

"Ramettan's eyes would burn on looking at sunlight," Amma told us.

We also echoed it by chanting in unison.

"Raman uncle's eyes would burn on looking at sunlight."

After a few weeks he reduced his food intake to just half a glass of milk and a small plantain.

Then from one *ekadasi* day (a sacred day for the Hindus) onwards he skipped that too, and demanded only half a glass of water containing a few basil leaves. Amma's eyes were filled with tears when she told us about it.

"I am frightened, children...," she held us close to her. "It is pitiful to see him."

The voice of Atma that came from his room was also becoming weaker and weaker...

Raman uncle's pathetic life came to an end at last on a Diwali day. When his body was taken to the funeral pyre Amma did not cry; nor did anyone of us. We believed that he had returned to his original self; the photo hanging on the wall.

After the ceremony of collecting his ashes and bones from the cremation ground, Amma opened the windows of the room used by him. When fresh air and sunlight flowed into the room hesitantly it seemed like a new world to us.

The gramophone was lying on the table as a relic of the past, an abandoned object. I noticed that Amma was looking at it with a slight fear.

"We lost our peace of mind ever since this damned thing was brought into this house," She reminded us. We nodded in agreement.

Actually what grieved us most was not our uncle's death, but the fact that we could no longer hear those songs from his room. Though they were full of pathos, they had become part of our dark and windy nights.

In a windy and rainy night that followed the observance of the sixteenth day of our uncle's death, Saigal's *"Soja Rajakumari..."* song was heard loudly from the neighbouring house where carpenter Joseph and his family were living. I closed my book and ran towards the window.

On hearing that distant sound, the flame of our kerosene lamp began to flicker again. Kitchu, the dog stood under the mango tree listening intently to the song. There was a hidden question in his eyes. How did this song cross over to that Joseph's house?

Amma had an answer for it.

"I gave the gramophone to Joseph. He is crazy about those old Hindi songs!"

However, our unhappiness about the loss of the gramophone and its songs did not last long, because when our younger uncle came on leave from Calcutta the next summer he brought a smaller music box. It was a radio made by the Grunding Company. Through that radio we heard the songs of Noorjahan, Talath Mohammed, Rafi, Latha Mangeshkar and Mukesh. In those days electricity was not available in our house. So the radio was played using batteries. On Wednesday nights we did our homework much earlier and waited eagerly for the 'Binaca Geetmala' programme and the mesmerising voice of its presenter Ameen Sayani. The programme was broadcast by the Radio Ceylon.

After a few months the usual chirpy voices of the children from Joseph's house ceased. The voices of Saigal, Mallik and Atma also mellowed. Kitchu gave up standing under the mango tree and retreated to the space under the eaves of the house.

Weeks later Joseph and his family came to our house to bid farewell to us. They had sold their house and the surrounding land so as to migrate to Malabar at the request of some of their relatives who had settled in Kuttiadi.

"Why are you leaving this place?" Our mother asked anxiously. "Your ancestors have lived here for generations."

"We have lost the ease of life, Ammoottiyamma," Joseph said in a worried voice.

His wife, who was standing behind him, came forward with the old gramophone in her hand.

"Keep it here, Ammoottiyamma. It is very difficult to carry it to Kuttiadi."

Amma stood dumbfounded for a moment. Meanwhile, Joseph and family rushed out without saying anything further.

While placing that gramophone back on the table in the southern room, my heart was brimming with excitement. Then I heard a sound outside the room. I raised my head and looked out of the window. Kitchu was standing there pressing his face against the window bars. His eyes were sparkling.

When I came out of the room and looked at the wall, I found Raman uncle in the ash-coloured coat and felt hat smiling at me for the first time.

There was not even a tinge of sadness on his face then.

Translation of Pāṭṭupeṭṭi

✦ ✦ ✦

12

A Vacation

They had come to spend their summer vacation with their grandmother—Kesavankutty's two children from Delhi, Malathi's youngest son from Mumbai and after a week, quite unexpectedly, Gopu's three children including the five year old Chinnan from the United States.

The grandmother's happiness knew no bounds. It was a family reunion after a long time. Children of diverse nature and of different ages have gathered under the same roof, like the different colours of a rainbow. She was thrilled at the thought that they were her own grandchildren—the youngest generation of her family.

However, such happy moments came to her life very rarely. One or the other of her children might come with family during alternate summer vacations. Most often she would not be given prior information regarding these visits, because they wanted to surprise her. They had all kinds of explanations to give on their inability to combine their visits together.

Vacations for schools and colleges vary from place to place and the companies and institutions where they work also had their own set of rules and schedules....

"Anyway, I'm happy that at last all of you could make it together," the mother heaved a sigh of relief. "You can spend your days here as you please; but leave the children to me. Devaki Amma and I will take care of them. While going outside the house Raman Nair will accompany them."

Her children laughed on seeing their mother brimming with excitement.

When the grandma and the grandchildren posed for a group photo near the platform where basil plants were grown for prosperity, Devaki Amma and Raman Nair joined them. They were also thrilled greatly. 'It is after a long time the big house has become noisy' they thought. Within no time the children messed up the courtyard, which was strewn with sand. They picked up shells of all shades and shapes from the compound and scattered them all over.

In the afternoon when the children insisted on going out the grandmother instructed Raman Nair with great concern:

"Keep a watchful eye on the children, Raman Nair. This place is quite unfamiliar to them."

On hearing it Girija, the eldest among the children, and Ajith and Arun, who were in their late teens, would laugh. She would not have shown this much concern about us if she had seen us crossing the busy roads of big cities with the body movements of a ballerina. Though Jimmy was just twelve years old, he was quite familiar with the busy traffic in some of the roads in Los Angeles.

While they were walking down the steps of the verandah the grandmother said from behind:

"Bring them back before it gets dark, Raman Nair; otherwise the children won't be able to see the path clearly. Take special care about the little ones. Keep hold of their hands always. They should not be allowed to run in the dark."

"Don't worry. I've taken a torch containing six cells." Raman Nair showed the torch tucked under one of his arms and the thick stick kept under the other.

"What is the stick for, Raman Nair?" Malathi asked.

"There will be some use with it in villages." Raman Nair smiled.

While climbing down the hill Raman Nair grasped Chinnan's hand; but the little one did not like it. When he tried to slip from his grip, he felt it getting tighter.

"The old man is nuts," Chinnan whispered to his sister Pinky, shrugging his shoulders. He wanted to run alone down the hill. And Pinky who was elder to him by three years was too happy to join him.

"Don't try to run down the hill, children. It is me that your grandmother will scold," Raman Nair said, tightening his grasp on Chinnan's hand further and grabbing Pinky's hand too in the meantime.

He did not see their sulky faces; nor did he hear them muttering something.

While sitting in front of the sacred oil lamp listening to the grandmother reading the Ramayana, the children had a lot of complaints to be made against Raman Nair. Kesavankutty's eldest daughter, Girija, who was a final year college student, acted as the translator between the other children and the grandmother. She alone among the children knew at least a little Malayalam, thanks to the hard work she put in at her father's insistence. The grandmother laughed showing her thin teeth when the children levelled their charges. She did not tell the children that Raman Nair was a mahout once and was habituated to tending unruly elephants. Though the old stick was still with him, she had no idea of what had happened to the hook he had used for controlling the elephants. 'Anyway, as he has ceased to be a mahout, why should he require a hook now? It cannot be used even for plucking mangoes,' she thought.

The next day the grandmother instructed Raman Nair not to be so strict with the children. "Everything is new here and they are celebrating their new-found freedom, like the birds released from their cages."

"The youngest one is rather unmanageable," Raman Nair laughed, putting his hand over his mouth.

"His father Gopu too was quite mischievous during his childhood. He had fallen from the mango tree and jackfruit tree, and had broken his arm or leg several times. God, what a headache he was! And there is no wonder that the children who live overseas, eating frogs, crabs, birds and all kinds of animals are rather unruly."

The children were provided sleeping arrangements alongside the grandmother's bed, in the outhouse on the southern side. The first two nights were quite amusing for the children, sleeping side by side on three beds put together... rolling from bed to bed and fighting each other with the pillows. It was a continuation of the fight they had in the afternoon, in the form of splashing water on one another while they were taking bath in the pool. Raman Nair had to plunge into the pool to make them stop it.

Anyway, on the third day the children raised some complaints:

"There's no TV and cable connection here."

"What a prickly heat! The power supply fails frequently. How can we stay here without A/C?"

"I feel eerie when the power supply fails in the night; almost like getting lost in an African forest."

"There's something unpleasant about this room and its walls; no ventilation and light."

"A kind of haunted feeling; isn't it, sister? I dare not look out of the window during the night. It's so dark outside."

"In the dead of night when everything is quiet outside, some frightening sounds are heard intermittently."

"That's the cry of insects, Jimmy."

"Then what is this 'crow, crow' sound?"

"That's frog, Pinky."

"'Frog' means?" Jimmy asked.

"I will show it to you near the pool tomorrow. Go to sleep now, baby"—Girija held him close to her and stroked him gently on the back.

"That's the cry of the frogs in the pool, children. They are crying for rain," the grandmother explained.

"Somebody told me that Raman Nair had an elephant. It must be a lie; isn't it, sister?"

"He was the mahout of the elephant that belonged to the prince's residence. It was a long time ago," the grandmother said.

"Did Raman Nair move from place to place on an elephant's back in those days?

"At times."

"Didn't he fall down?"

"He was very much experienced in sitting on an elephant's back."

"Sleep eludes me, didi," Arun was heard telling Girija.

"Why?"

"Some sort of uneasiness."

"Are you afraid to sleep here? What a shame! Don't forget that you are a plus-two student."

"Some strange sounds are heard during the sleep—something like the sound of anklets...the footsteps of somebody walking gently...," Ajith said.

"The trouble with you people is that you have seen so many Hindi movies. Your Bollywood directors are so fond of converting such old country houses into haunted houses."

"No, didi; it was not just a hallucination. I really heard the sounds last night."

"I too."

"Just as in the movie, a woman in white sari, with long hair was taking a stroll in the garden. Her movement was something like a catwalk, with her anklets tinkling," Girija laughed.

"Yeah...yeah..."

"And hidden behind a thicket, Latha Mangeshkar was singing aloud."

"You make a joke of everything, sister; but this is true—this eerie feeling."

"Did you really hear the sounds, children?"—The grandmother raised her head from the pillow and lay on a side of her body, resting her head on her hand.

"Yes, grandma," everybody except Girija said in one accord.

After a short while Chinnan changed sides and said sadly:

"I didn't hear anything."

"It's all lies, baby," Girija whispered in his ears. "As you three haven't seen Hindi movies, you won't be able to hear it."

Though he did not understand what she said, he grunted something and slipped into sleep soon.

"I have asked Raman Nair to make you all pass through an elephant's legs so that you will be rid of all such unwanted fears. However, elephants are seen very rarely in this area these days. Hence Raman Nair may not be able to arrange it that easily. In that case, I will ask the oracle to tie charmed strings or talismans on your arms."

"There's no need of it, grandma. Everything is their hallucination," Girija said trying to suppress her laughter.

"Did you really hear Latha Mangeshkar singing?" the grandmother persisted.

Arun alone uttered the word 'yes' this time.

"It might be Ammuvedathy. She was very fond of songs," the grandmother said, recollecting something.

"Go to sleep, grandma. It's very late already," Girija said.

When the entire family assembled in the dining room adjacent to the kitchen for breakfast, Malathi said:

"Now the children have started making all sorts of complaints. When they start pointing out the facilities that are not available in this house, the list looks pretty long. And if you go through that list, you will find that there is practically nothing left in this house."

"Don't forget that we were all born and brought up in this very house with all its inadequacies and have become what we are today," Gopu said.

"We grew up almost like chickens, goats and ducks," Kesavankutty remarked. "I studied in a govt. school with very poor academic standard. The medium of instruction was Malayalam. Still I could become the only candidate to get a first class among the 20% students who passed the matriculation in our batch.

"Though we studied in Malayalam schools, it hasn't caused much difficulty in building up our careers," Gopu asserted. "I can communicate well in English even to the Americans."

"We were determined to learn English and we succeeded in it; but it is quite horrible to hear the butler's English spoken by the 'twinkle, twinkle' generation."

The grandmother was lost in memory.

"Life was quite thrilling when ours was a huge undivided family. Bhageerathy and her children; Sumathy and her children; Kumarettan, Janu and their children; and Ammuvedathy as the leader—all lived together under the same roof. What a jolly time it was! The grown-ups would have entertainments like *antakshari,* with poems of well-known poets; elders will either sing Kathakali songs or play the local version of chess. However, playing of cards was forbidden by the eldest uncle. The boys would go into the open ground in front of the temple and play various games till noon until they are called for lunch. In addition to the members of the family there would also be some outsiders to have lunch here. Don't think that it was a grand feast. Some kind of dishes would be prepared using the yam, millet and various kinds of tubers cultivated in our own farm. During the season of mango and jackfruit they will be cooked in different ways and served for breakfast, lunch and supper."

"But grandma, things have changed a lot," Kesavankutty's son Ajith pointed out. "Life has become very fast now. Everybody is running short of time."

"Don't talk about shortage of time, son. Both Bill Clinton and Raman Nair have the same twenty four hours for a day. Both of them have the same Sun and the same night. How you utilise the time is what matters," Gopu interrupted.

"As Girija, Arun and Ajith are older than the others and are in their late teens, let me ask them a simple question. Do you like this countryside?" The question came from Kesavankutty.

They did not give an immediate answer to that question; but exchanged furtive glances.

"Look, I want a frank answer." Kesavankutty insisted.

After a while Ajith said:

"This place is okay for short holidays, that too occasionally. Beyond that.... No, it would be very difficult."

"True; just one week... or two weeks at most. To stay here further will be highly boring."

"So, for Arun and Ajith this is not a bad place for spending a vacation; some sort of a picnic spot. What about you, Girija?"

"I like this village very much," Girija said, hugging the grandmother. "I really love this place and everything found here."

"She is simply bluffing. If you really like this countryside, let me ask you a question, sister, will you marry somebody from here?"

Girija felt a little embarrassed and said hesitantly:

"No..."

"Why?" her father asked.

"That doesn't look good."

"Why?" Malathi laughed.

"That will create problems, aunty. It will be very difficult to adjust to the situations here."

"I was transplanted from Kolkata to this countryside after my marriage. Still I could adjust well to the life here. Then why can't you?" Her mother asked.

"She must have already chosen somebody—a Punjabi or one from UP."

"No, never. I will marry only a Malayali; from our own caste. But he should be one settled outside Kerala; with at least a basic knowledge of Malayalam like me."

"Why so many conditions?"

"Life will be boring otherwise. Some kind of compatibility problem too."

"See how today's children think, mother? They have their own opinions about everything, and well thought out plans and ideas. More importantly, they have no inhibitions about telling them openly to elders. It's no use trying to impose others' opinions on them. Their brains have grown double their age," Kesavankutty said.

"Why not?"—the question came from the five year old Chinnan.

"You little hero...!" Malathi pinched his earlobe playfully.

"You know, in America this Chinnan could get me arrested quite easily. If he picks up the phone, dial a particular number and complain about ill-treatment by parents, the cops would rush into our house within no time," Gopu said.

"No, I'm not that naughty, pop..." Chinnan grunted.

"An angry young man," Malathi commented.

"He blackmails me sometimes threatening about the police. The hard disk inside their brains is overflowing with junk data. They know much more than what I knew when I passed out of the school at the age of fifteen."

"It's not funny, pop!" Chinnan grunted again, expressing his dislike.

"These kids are always floating in the cyberspace now. There is practically nothing unknown to them."

"By the way, how did his elder brother become 'Jimmy' all of a sudden?" Malathi asked. "He was Narayanankutty even at the time of his last visit here. Mother gave him that sacred name after the eldest uncle."

He threw that name away. He said he could not bear that heavy name. And he himself chose the name 'Jimmy'. It is very easy to call that name."

"It is a name given to dogs here," the grandmother laughed.

"Shit."

"Children themselves choose the names for them? *Siva, Siva*!"—the grandmother could not believe it.

"It is good Jimmy," Kesavankutty patted Jimmy on the back. "I like your openness. This is what we lacked. We didn't have the courage to open our mouths in front of our fearsome uncles. We would just mumble to them from behind. Here we are all good friends and talk things openly. This openness is something good. It will help us understand one another. However, there are certain things that are purely our own. They are so dear to us that we cannot give them up. I like Girija's stand that she will marry only a Malayali. That's an interesting idea. It reflects her desire to confine herself to our own little culture...."

The children were listening with great interest.

Kesavankutty continued:

"You should also know how we people lived in our younger days. You cannot even imagine such a life. Now you are talking about AC and internet. I studied my lessons in the light of a kerosene lamp when I was a college student. When it was time to prepare for the examinations, I would go to the southern veranda with a small kerosene lamp. The unbearable heat in the month of *Chaithram* and the swarming mosquitos made it impossible to sit and study somewhere inside the house. Reading for a long time in that faint light would make my eyes ache. Electricity became available in this area many years after the completion of my M A course."

Unable to believe what Kesavankutty said, the children looked at one another.

"Without light...?"

"Without fan...?"

"Without TV...?"

"When you look at these things from your cyberspace everything appears quite weird, don't they?

"Though I did my M.Sc, years after ettan's college days, it was a real ordeal for me to go to college," Malathi said. "I had to walk five miles to reach the bus stop in front of the temple. Then I had to change two buses to reach the college. Hence I was always late. The moment I entered the class room, the teacher's face would flush furiously. I was allowed to continue in the college only because I was a bright student."

"Why didn't you buy a moped, Mummy?"

"To buy a moped...!" Malathi laughed. "There was no such thing here in those days. And even if it was available, the elders in the house wouldn't allow the girls to ride it. Besides, of the five miles I had to walk, half a mile was through a paddy field. Walking along the narrow ridge in the field required the skill of a circus artist. During the rainy season the entire paddy field would be submerged by water. Then I would have to walk along a roundabout path, which increased the distance by two more miles."

The children could not believe what Malathi said. The furtive glances they exchanged implied that it was just a concocted story aimed at impressing them.

"When I submitted the application for the M.Sc course the Professor told me: 'You will be given admission here; but you cannot be a day scholar. You should stay in the hostel. Post-graduation is not child's play. Besides, you will have to spend a lot of time in the lab to finish your practical lessons. Hence you are likely to leave the college vey late in the evening.'

"Then followed the funny episode. Just like the villain character in kathakali the eldest uncle came near the curtain and roared: 'Girls from this family should not think of staying at a hostel!' The whole house shook violently. Luckily for us, it didn't collapse. Our mother also stood by him with all the support." Gopu added.

The grandmother laughed gently.

"Those were the days, children. No girl from our family had stayed alone outside the house. All were scared of going against the traditions and do unaccustomed things. But I must say one thing; what the elders say may look unacceptable at first; but later on you will realise that there is a lot of sense in it."

"Though you were forced to be a day scholar, it hasn't done any harm to you," Kesavankutty laughed. "Thanks to the hard journey to the college, you could reduce your obesity. What a clumsy shape you had in your school days!"

"I know, your instigation was also there behind mother's adamant stand," Malathi said in a complaining tone. "I know you were prompted by jealousy. You had to complete your college education in the faint light of a kerosene lamp, fighting with mosquitos; then why should this girl should be allowed to enjoy the privilege of staying at the college hostel in the town?"

"If you had stayed at the hostel, would you have obtained a better M.Sc. degree? The M.Sc. that you have is enough for teaching at the college, cooking rice and managing the household affairs."

Kesavankutty's resounding laugh had close resemblance to that of the younger uncle.

"Wasn't teaching at the college always secondary to cooking?" Malathi was getting angry.

"Why, is there a doubt now? Isn't it how your daily routine has been scheduled?" her husband, Unniyettan laughed.

"M.C.P," Girija whispered. "All men are M.C.P."

"Shit," Jimmy murmured.

"I don't know in which age people like Unni uncle are living," Arun expressed his displeasure.

The grandmother intervened at this juncture:

"Don't argue with each other, children. Nobility and family reputation are not the things you can buy with money."

"What is this thing called 'nobility', sister?" Pinky whispered in Girija's ears.

"Though I have heard of it often from the elders, I don't know the meaning myself."

"How can the Americans understand the meaning of nobility?" Gopu said. "It is a country of immigrants. If aristocracy is a burden for the British, money power reigns supreme in America. The richest is the noblest."

"Nonsense! You guys are still to get out of the hangover of the feudal period. Though the world has changed a lot and the isolated voices of women are being echoed the world over, you still foster a lot of antiquated notions. Nostalgia is an exciting thing in the old age; but don't try to pass it on to the younger generation. Let them grow up with an open mind and with fewer chains."

"This is not just nostalgia, Malathi. We can have changes in the old value system, but why should we insist on demolishing them totally? Kesavankutty asked.

"Why do you use such tough words, brother? The children won't understand your language. Can't you leave them alone? Let them embrace and enjoy the life they see around them. What is wrong in it?"

"Teaching children for years have made our teacher a staunch supporter of them, apart from being a self-proclaimed feminist." Gopu teased Malathi.

"We are all on their side," Kesavankutty burst into laughter. "Still, there are certain things which need to be told to them. And they have the ability to choose between what they need and what are to be rejected."

The children were amused at the heated arguments between the elders. After a while the little Jimmy asked in a low voice:

"What's this feudal hangover?"

"Perhaps the worst kind of hangover." Malathi could not control herself. She was still excited about the levels the exchanges had taken her.

"Then, what is this hangover?" Jimmy was visibly confused.

"I don't know," Girija pleaded her ignorance.

"Whatever you say, it is a fact that the westerners have begun to think sociologically about the good aspects of our joint family system. Concepts, such as, family life and the necessity of nurturing children within the house by their own loving parents are being discussed everywhere. In fact, it is man's selfishness that has led us to the nuclear family system. We don't have the tolerance to coexist with others; nor are we prepared to give up even our little comforts. Making compromises is unthinkable to us. The westerners don't know anything about the institution of family. Then how will they have things like tradition, nobility, and dignity? When the children grow up they will find out their own means of livelihood and shift to separate apartments, if possible. What those islets lack is the bond of love," Gopu said.

"In a joint family you have a number of cousins and relatives, all living under one roof, sharing your joys and sorrows and trying to support each other...."

"Enough...Enough," Arun butted in. "You people are spoiling our vacation," He whimpered.

"Forget it, young man. What you said is true," Kesavankutty patted Arun on the back. "The company of the grown-ups is highly boring, isn't it? So, let's talk about something interesting; something very crazy. But I don't know which things are interesting to you people. The craze of you and I may be different."

"Daddy, please leave us alone," Girija requested.

When the children went outside after breakfast, Kesavankutty said:

"We brainwashed them a lot, didn't we?"

"Brainwashing them? Impossible! They will make you accept their ideas instead. I have been handling these types of guys at the college for the last so many years. At the beginning of each academic year, when a new batch of students appear before me I am convinced that they are smarter than their immediate predecessors. It may be Laws of the Nature; the new generation has to be smarter than the old one to survive in a world which is getting more and more complicated day by day."

They were not aware of the passing of days. It was only when they began to pack their bags one afternoon, the grandmother realised sadly that those twenty days had the duration of only a single day.

"We have become some sort of guests; aren't we, mother?" Kesavankutty asked in a low vice, without looking at the mother's face.

The mother could not say anything, because a sob caught in her throat.

"Don't worry, we shall come again, and spend some time together like this."

The mother knew very well that it was a vain promise. As she was well aware of the endlessness of waiting, she never waited for anybody. And quite unexpectedly one or the other of her children would turn up on the doorstep, calling out 'mother'.

The mother was quite sure that she would not witness another get-together like this. Hence a number of photos of the children and the grandchildren posing together were taken at her request so as to be preserved in the album.

"The reunion and the parting seem to have occurred in a short time," somebody said.

'For me it was a flow of mercy from the sky, quite unexpectedly.'—the mother thought.

Children's faces were also unusually gloomy. They stood around the grandmother.

"Savithri's parents always complain that we do not stay with them even for two days. As their house is in a town, children like staying there," Gopu said looking somewhere.

"Yes, yes," the grandmother nodded her head. "They too have as much right as that of me over the children." Her voice quivered.

Kesavankutty's face dropped. He glanced at Radha's face.

While bidding farewell to the mother every time, he would try to have a smile on his face, and wouldn't look her in the eyes.

However, every face looked glum this time. They were painfully aware that it would take a long time for another reunion.

Anyway, Kesavankutty managed to say:

"Don't worry, mother. Next year also we will come, after planning everything in advance. And there's ample time for planning things."

Gopu kept silent. Though this joint homecoming was quite accidental, was it ominous of anything?—he feared.

Malathi gave a dubious 'hmm'.

The grandmother knew very well that it was a hollow promise. She simply nodded her head.

It is better not to tell me in advance, children. If I keep on waiting and you don't turn up that will be unbearable to me—she thought.

"If only I could see at least my grandchildren occasionally. I may not be able to talk to them properly, but just to see them...."

Kesavankutty burst out laughing so as to ease the tension.

"Listen, Amma doesn't want us now; she would like to have the company of her grandchildren alone."

"Can old people say so?" the grandmother' eyes filled with tears. "Children, grandchildren, other relatives, neighbours and even passers-by are needed in the old age. Nobody can be avoided."

Malathi looked at her watch.

"It's time for you to leave for the station, *etta*," she reminded Kesavankutty.

Kesavankutty nodded.

Suddenly Girija came forward, bent before the grandmother and touched her feet. Then Ajith followed suit. The grandmother was shaken for a while. It was the first time the children were doing such a thing.

Arun too prostrated at the grandmother's feet, though he did not know what exactly he was doing.

Then Jimmy and Pinky followed the others mechanically.

When the little Chinnan walked slowly towards the grandmother, she prevented him from bending before her; she hugged him instead and pressed her lips at the crown of his head. Her eyes were full of tears.

"Don't prevent him, mother. The children did it of their own accord. We hadn't asked them to do so," she heard Kesavankutty's quivering voice. "Now we have only these things to be given to you, mother; and I pray that we should have at least these privileges retained."

The grandmother wiped the tears from her eyes and tried to smile.

Translation of O<u>l</u>ivukālaṃ

✦ ✦ ✦

13

Distant Views

In a cold and misty morning, a man called Bhagyanathan was looking at the street below from the narrow balcony of his flat on the sixth floor of the building.

It has been his habit for years to wake up before sunrise and stand on the balcony, looking at the street. Many years ago, when those skyscrapers and the narrow pathways in between were not there, the balcony overlooked the sea. In those days he could see the waves breaking on the shore and the dark overcast sky covering the entire area with a thick blanket during the rainy season. Later on, those concrete buildings which came up one after the other hid the sea and those precious views from him. Still he came to the balcony every morning before the streets woke up, in order to hear the whispering sounds of the sea from faraway.

Though the street was quiet generally with very few pedestrians on it, it looked a little too noisy that morning. When he watched closely, he could see somebody lying on the verandah of the beauty parlour on the opposite side of the street. A few people were crowding around the body.

He suspected that it was a woman. Why people had crowded around her, he wondered. A faceless woman sleeping on the verandah of a shop in this faceless city—there was nothing unusual about it. It's not surprising either, even if the woman was naked.

Anyway, he felt a little uneasy; a needless fear crept into him.

"Son...," he called out, looking into his flat.

"Why, Dad?" his son, a college student, responded to his call, unmoved from his bed?

"Fetch me the binoculars."

"What for? To watch the sea?" It was his wife's lazy voice, followed by a long yawn. She too was in the bed, under a blanket.

Returning to his bedroom Bhagyanathan took the binoculars from the shelf and returned to the balcony again.

'Has the crowd swelled?'

He brought the binoculars closer to his eyes.

Large waves were moving across the sea under the dark shadows of the ash-coloured clouds. The rising waves collapsed soon and escaped towards the shore. On reaching the shore, they spit mouthfuls of foam and crawled back into the sea....

For a moment, his fingers trembled and he failed to focus the binoculars onto the scene in the street. Exasperated, he put it down and looked with naked eyes again.

'Yes, it is a woman. It seems that she is wearing a red sari. Is she lying on her front? The crowd which has gathered around her like ants have hidden her almost completely.'

What had happened to that faceless woman in red sari?

Who was she? A beggar, a madwoman, a prostitute, or a villager who came to the city seeking her livelihood?

Darkness receded completely and the morning sunlight spread everywhere. The shadow of his building covered the entire street. Vehicles began to roar.

Still he could not see clearly what was happening in the street.

He took the binoculars again.

After lingering for some time on the crests of the waves formed in the centre of the sea, the red morning sunlight was seen scattering and dissolving in water. The boy in red shirt, who was trying to make the model of a house on the brink of the shore, was scared to see a wave rushing onto him and ran away with a yell.

"Son...," he peeped inside and called out helplessly; but there was no reply.

After a while his wife came out in her night clothes, rubbing her eyes.

"Don't disturb him—the poor boy. Let him sleep," she said with some irritation. "What do you want?"

Holding onto the railing of the balcony he pointed to the street.

"Why is a commotion there?" he asked.

Looking at the crowd intently his wife said in an emotionless voice:

"Yet another suicide!" Her voice was casual.

He shuddered at the thought of suicide.

"Why? What for?"

"Perhaps somebody must have raped her last night."

His wife leaned to the railing of the balcony and turned her eyes towards the labourers working inside the skeleton of a huge building coming up at the end of the street. They looked like moving lines of ants.

"The Telugu labourers working on that building have camped somewhere in that compound. She must be one among them."

She added after a while:

"Maybe somebody's daughter."

"Or wife...mother...younger sister...elder sister..." He muttered.

"Who knows?"

"Anyway, I can't see it properly."

Handing the binoculars to her he implored:

"Please focus it properly and tell me what exactly is happening there."

When she began to look through the binoculars he asked anxiously:

"Can you see clearly?"

"Yeah."

"What do you see?"

"Nothing particular. Certainly not what you see."

"What else, then?"

"The normal things I see usually."

"Eh?"

"The racecourse at Mahalakshmi, the horses galloping madly on the final lap, the jockeys in striped shirts and red caps, crouching on the backs of the galloping horses, the shouting crowd, the flying hats, ice cream cups.... It's fantastic...."

"Stop it."

When he seized the binoculars from her, she lost the sight of the racecourse.

The sun has risen high. Still the shadow of his building seemed unwilling to recede from the street.

The crowd in front of the beauty parlour had increased. 'Is the man in khaki dress leaning on a bicycle a watchman of the building? Why the police haven't turned up yet?'

"I don't think it is rape or suicide," His wife was disinterested. "Such incidents are quite common here, dear. Hence people won't waste their time hanging on to it; they have better things to do on a busy working day morning. You know the kind of crowd in the local trains during the busy hours and bus queues are none better."

"What could it be then?"

"It should be murder; that is why people have gathered there in large numbers. I could see some blood stains on the wall."

He was startled to hear the word 'murder'. Why, why was she murdered? Were the people crowded there her fellow workers?

Tightening the string of his pyjama he said:

"Let me go downstairs to see what has happened actually."

"Are you mad?" his wife laughed aloud. "Do you know what the time is now? Don't you want to take bath in hot water, have breakfast and do some office work at home?"

"There's ample time to do all these."

"Have you forgotten that the lift is not working? That is the reason you gave application to your boss for permission to work from home."

"It doesn't matter."

"Hasn't the doctor warned you against climbing the steps?"

"I don't care."

"Don't be silly."

Visibly agitated, she called out to her son, who was still asleep. After a couple of attempts the boy came out, muttering something and rubbing his eyes.

"What, Mummy, why do you disturb me like this? Don't you know that our college is closed today." His voice was rough.

"Look, son.... Your Dad is batty. He wants to go downstairs. A beggar-woman is lying dead on the verandah of a shop. He wants to have a look at her. How crazy!"

"The old man is nuts these days," The boy expressed his annoyance at being roused from his sleep. Looking at the street from the balcony he growled: "Some bloody whore...."

The father did not stop him from using such foul words. He had reached the front door. His wife rushed after him.

"Look dear, this is too much. It is me that the doctor uncle will scold," she said impatiently.

Without looking back, he tried to hum a tune. A long forgotten song of Noorjehan.

Before his wife could catch up with him he had climbed down a few steps. Panting lightly, he moved towards the glass door of the lift on the landing and peeped inside. It seemed to him that he was standing on the brink of an abyss with some black ropes hanging down from a square cage. For a moment, he felt giddy and exhausted. Sweating and panting heavily, he looked upwards helplessly. Standing near the upper landing, his wife and son were watching his movements with utter disbelief.

Suddenly his son ran down the stairs, grabbed his hand and said:

"Come, Dad. Let's go upstairs."

Clinging on to his son's hands desperately and holding the railing tightly with the other, he began to climb the steps. He was breathing heavily. He did not have the courage to face his wife's furious looks.

"Slowly, son, slowly! Be careful!" She yelled from the top of the stairs.

Hanging on to the son's shoulders like a small child....

How sturdy and warm his shoulders have grown, he wondered. My darling son—the kid who used to swing onto my hand!

He sank into the sofa. The old fan began to revolve with a groan.

"Didn't I tell you not to climb down the stairs? How many times had the doctor uncle warned you, that you should not step out of the door. You think you are still young."

Though he thought of asking her whether he had become an old man at the age of fifty five, nothing came out of his mouth. With a bewildered look on the face, he kept staring at the sparkling red ring at the centre of the fan.

His son was standing on the balcony.

"Look Mummy, a jeep has come there. I think the police have arrived."

"As I said earlier, it must be suicide or a murder," his mother said.

"Look through the binoculars and tell me what happens there actually," Bhagyanathan beseeched his son in a tired voice.

"OK, Dad."

Opening his mouth, he gulped two or three mouthfuls of the moist air thrown by the blades of the fan, and wet his lips with his tongue.

His son returned from the balcony and put the binoculars on the table. When he began to comb his hair without saying anything, his father asked him eagerly:

"Could you see it properly?"

"Yeah," the son said casually.

"What is it?"

"Sachin Tendulkar. He was sweeping the ball to the mid-wicket, keeping his left leg raised a little. How stylish! You should see his shoulders and arms! Had I been blessed with such shoulders and wrists, I would have scaled the heights of cricket."

The father felt breathless. He rose to his feet slowly, took his binoculars and staggered onto the balcony.

"What are you doing?" Can't you take some rest? Shall I call the doctor?" his wife shouted reproachfully; but he did not listen to her.

He brought the lenses close to his eyes.

My sea and my favourite views, all hidden by this monstrous structures. New high-rise buildings competing with each other to touch the skies first.

'Is it getting dark outside suddenly? Is it going to rain again? The grey clouds scattered all over the sky have all gathered together to take the shape of thick black canopy.'

Darkness had already started melting into the waves. It was now crawling onto the shore covering everything on the way—treetops, lamp posts, deserted roads, isolated pedestrians....

He, the man called Bhagyanathan shut his eyes slowly.

Translation of Dūrakkāḻcakaḷ

✦ ✦ ✦

14

The Generations

Though the morning sunlight had spread everywhere it was slightly cold outside. On reaching the arrival lounge with a heavy suitcase, he was quite surprised to see Lekha there. He had not expected that she would come. She was sitting curled up on a chair, wrapped up in a shawl. She did not even stir when he went near her.

"Morning, daughter. A real surprise!" He put his hand on her shoulder. "I never thought you would come."

Lekha rose to her feet slowly. She looked distracted. While walking towards the door leading to the corridor he said:

"I couldn't sleep last night. I had gone to bed very late and had to wake up at around 3.30 to catch the early morning flight. I feared that I would oversleep. Besides, the weather was a bit too cold and sleep eluded me."

Even while moving towards the car Lekha did not say anything and kept her face lowered. When she seated herself in the driving seat of the car, he suppressed a smile and got into the car. After pushing the suitcase to the rear of the car he put his hand on her shoulder again.

"Come on dear, what happened; you look so serious today. I never thought you would come alone all this way, driving the car. You should not have sent the driver back."

She started the car. While driving past a row of vehicles parked there she suddenly increased the speed, quite unusually for her.

With a view to making her say something he said:

"I tried to contact you twice or thrice last night, but the cell was switched off. And nobody picked up the landline phone."

She kept silent again.

'It is better to wait until she cools down,' he thought.

After driving for some time, she stirred a little and smoothed her disheveled hair. Pulling up suddenly at the red light she asked:

"Daddy, why did you go to Delhi?"

He paused for a moment and laughed aloud.

"It's long since I visited the Kutubminar; I wanted to check whether it has grown further."

She looked at him angrily.

"I've told you already—an unexpected company meeting and some delayed business visits." He explained hurriedly.

"Nothing else?"

"No, nothing in particular. See, if there was anything else, I wouldn't have made the trip, exposing myself to the freezing cold in Delhi."

"To attend the company meeting!" she raised her voice. "Concocting false reasons for a trip is quite easy for you people."

He stretched out his hand to put it again on her shoulder; but she moved aside suddenly and kept staring at the road. After a while she increased the speed and muttered:

"Maya came to see me yesterday. She was crying like a baby."

Though a little embarrassed, he managed a weak smile and commented:

"Occasional cries are good for girls of your age. It works as a purifier."

"Don't be so cruel, dad."

"And what did Maya say?"

He noticed her face redden suddenly.

"Look, daddy; No need for a hide-and-seek game between us. I know why you went to Delhi. I know everything. Still, I can't believe that you could be so cruel...."

"What do you mean?"

"Enough, daddy; stop this cheap game. It is not suited to you. What are you going to gain by putting obstacles in that poor girl's marriage? The moment I got a hint of your move, I asked you not to interfere in it and to leave them alone."

He turned uncomfortably in the seat, with the uneasiness of a child whose falsehood has been detected unexpectedly:

"You children don't know about the relationship between Maya's father and me; a generation born and brought up in the villages with limited facilities. It is something well outside the orbit of the cyber generation of city-dwellers who live in the midst of all the comforts and luxuries. What you are familiar with are the stereo-types of relationships. For me Maya is another daughter like you. Hence I cannot bear to see her running into trouble recklessly."

"What trouble?" Lekha burst out.

Slowing the car down to a halt on the left side of the road, she went on: "Is there anything wrong in being in love with a man of her choice? Or that she herself has decided with whom she should live? She is not an emotional or impetuous character as you think. She is quite capable of distinguishing between good and bad. And to speak about her friend, he is...."

"This is not just a case of friendship, dear. It's much more than that. A question of living a whole long life together amidst all kinds of odds and discords. She and her partner will not be alone in their world. There are many other factors which would come in automatically when you think of a family as such. It is a group of people, known and unknown, close and distant who complete the picture of a family. There are several apparent contradictions between Maya and her lover. Hence they will have to make a plethora of compromises, if they want to live peacefully under the same roof. Once the initial zest dies down, discord and disharmony will arise.... It is not the caste factor alone, although it would still remain as a major irritant throughout their life particularly in a society like ours. Again a whole lot of other issues like family background, grooming, lifestyles, approach towards life etc. would crop up in between. The burden of sacrifices to be made would go on increasing as the days progress."

"It is quite surprising to hear these antiquated words from your mouth, daddy. What happened to my old daddy? I can't believe this change. If things are as simple as you said now, all the love marriages should end in failure, and the marriages arranged by the elders after ensuring that the horoscopes match should turn out successful; but is it always só, daddy?"

He did not reply, and she continued after a while:

"Anyway, they have decided to take the plunge after giving a lot of thought to all these aspects. Besides, his father has given all his blessings to the marriage. However, daddy and Maya's father Kurup uncle won't understand the intensity of their relationship."

"I don't blame Maya. People of your age are very short-sighted on such matters. We have seen the world a lot. So when you people are seen going astray...."

"Going astray! These are all dialogues heard in some old black and white movies. Do you think that the oldies with the reputation of inhabiting this world for decades are repositories of all wisdom? What you people do actually is to impose your own likes, dislikes and petty prejudices on others, particularly on the younger generation. The faces in the old family photos hanging on the walls of daddy's ancestral home may be imparting strength to you; but I have never had such an experience. And I don't want to become one among those photos with a moth-eaten face."

He leant back in the seat and lit a cigarette. On taking a few puffs he began to cough.

When the cough subsided he said:

"Look Lekha, I don't want to argue with you. I gave you a lot of freedom from childhood onwards. That's why you can say all these to my face. Anyway, start the car. Let's avoid quarrelling on the roadside."

"I'm sorry, daddy! You always say that we are good friends, and that's why I spoke so frankly...," she muttered while starting the car.

"Let me ask you something," he said, looking into her eyes. "Why are you so much interested in this case? Any special reason, apart from supporting your friend?"

She became a little embarrassed.

"Why did you ask me so, daddy?"

"Just a casual question...."

"No, there's something behind the question."

"Oh, nothing."

She fell silent, lost in some thoughts. Suddenly her face was seen blushing. Her father continued:

"There's no doubt that we are good friends; but in a family each person has a specific role to play and everybody is bound to preserve the sanctity and the limits of these roles. Though the joint family system has almost ceased to exist, the so-called nuclear unit comprising father, mother and children still remains intact, thanks to the backing of certain beliefs that run in our blood. Tradition is not such a bad thing. It is not a liability, but a possibility and strength. While standing before the photos you mentioned just now I hear my forefathers, seen and unseen, who lived decades ago, whispering to me. Many of the photographs taken in later years have become blurred; but the eyes in those brown photos talk to me a lot still."

He paused for throwing the cigarette butt away and continued:

"There's an old friend of mine, a senior scientist working for NASA. He has been in US for the last thirty years; a typical American citizen outside his apartment. But the moment he is inside it, and gets into the usual dhoti he is transformed into a typical villager from Kerala. When his daughter reached marriageable age he laid only two conditions—the bridegroom should be a man of noble birth and a Syrian Christian. Look dear, the concept of 'noble birth' is not such a bad thing."

"Nonsense! Whether at NASA or Sreeharikkotta, we launch a rocket only after performing the religious ritual of breaking the coconut on the ground."

"Certainly. And it's a fact that all of us do break coconuts, at least in our minds, whenever we venture into something important. There's nothing to be ashamed of, in confessing it."

"Ridiculous!" Lekha snorted contemptuously and fell silent.

Traffic had become heavy. Vehicles were running fast along the four-lane highway. Lekha was surprised that even in this faceless city, where people do not recognise each other, there are some small-minded people.

After some time she said gently, looking somewhere in the distance:

"I think you have intimidated that boy's father, a villager from Odisha, haven't you daddy?"

"Why should I intimidate him? Who am I to do it? And what wrong has he done?"

"You are all highly influential people and he is just a clerk in some government department. However, it so happened that he has got a smart son."

"There's no question of intimidation here." He was irritated visibly. "I just tried to put things in the proper perspective to him and asked him whether he thought it proper to approve of the alliance which would be equally unsuitable to both the boy and the girl."

"How can you say that Maya and her lover are unsuited to each other?"

"Look Lekha, if you think it is your duty to help your friend Maya, I have every right to apply the same to her father."

"If they disobey you...?"

"Let us see whether they will obey or not."

"Daddy, you know very well that the law of the country is on their side. If they are determined to get married you and Kurup uncle won't be able to prevent it. Moreover, if it becomes a court case, that will be shameful to Kurup uncle himself. I am surprised that you don't understand us the least. I don't believe in vague expressions like 'generation gap'. The reason why we don't understand each other may be the difference in outlooks regarding the value systems your generation is familiar with. You try to see everything through a very old pair of coloured lenses...."

He looked at his daughter in surprise. He had never expected such boldness from her. 'She has grown far beyond my estimation,' He thought. 'It is not she alone who speaks to me now. A number of girls like her, including Maya, are speaking out in one voice through her: "you don't understand us and vice versa".'

"In a sense what you said is true. I have no doubt that your generation is much more smarter than ours. That is a natural law. Life becomes more complicated with the passing of each generation; and Nature creates smarter people capable of tackling all such complexities."

"This is not a question of smartness, daddy; but one of clear vision. If you are blind to the changing ways and attitudes of the society, you will be very late in realising them."

"You might have read that change is the only thing that remains unchanged. But life will teach you that there are certain things that can never be changed."

"That is just a false notion."

"Not a false notion. There is a growing tendency all over the world to recover many of the things that were thrown away ages ago."

"Just a nostalgia, isn't it?"

"Not at all. There are some fundamental elements lying at the bottom of our hearts. I don't want to spoil their charm by giving them specific names."

"If you don't get angry let me ask you something, daddy."

She stared into his eyes and continued:

"If I were in Maya's position, what would be your stand?"

"Just the same, dear, because both of you are alike to me," he said firmly. "I was waiting for this question to come out of your mouth any moment. I have also envisaged the possibility you mentioned, on seeing the lifestyle of the people in this big city. This incident may be a rehearsal for facing such a trying situation later."

"Why did you give me a lot of freedom still?"

"What is the use of depriving you of your freedom? And I am sure that you know me better than anyone else."

"That means, you believe that I won't do anything against your wish; don't you, daddy?"

"Yes."

"Isn't it petty selfishness?"

"Yes; and such selfish notions are very dear to me."

"From childhood onwards you had been my greatest hero; a complete man in every sense, with a big mind. But I'm sorry to say that now you have become very small in my mind. It's time for you to get out of your Bohemian mask and intellectual halo, daddy. You are simply making pretensions before others.

Your wide reading, art exhibitions, *mushairas*, friendship with pipe smoking bearded men....It's all a mere show. You are still a feudal Nair from Annamanada at heart. All your outward show is intended to trick others. When it comes to your personal choices, you have an inflexible framework; and are quite unwilling to cross its bounds...."

"Enough Lekha, enough. You are transgressing all the limits," her father raised his voice.

"The daughters of Annamanada Nairs do not dare to say this much to their fathers, do they?"

"Enough, Lekha; stop it."

"Enough for me as well. This is not a question of generation gap; but a clear case of double-dealing. Nothing but hypocrisy. I hate it."

Her voice became hoarse suddenly, as if some kind of unknown bitterness was surging up from the deep recesses of her mind. She wanted to give vent to a host of feelings in a violent outburst.... Long forgotten rage towards her own hesitant lover, who retreated at the last moment; the resentment against his weak and cowardly father; the annoyance against her daddy, Kurup uncle and even Maya, who had dragged her into that relationship.

'They are all jointly playing some trick'—she thought. They spoke about great things initially; but now all of them are trying to be in the good books of each other. Poor Lekha alone was isolated.

She felt that something had choked her throat. Unable to utter anything she began to pant.

Without paying attention to his daughter, her father took his hand off her shoulder and sat closer to the door. From the big heap of memories he could now dust off the picture of a three year old girl staring in bewilderment at the body of her mother that was laid on the floor, wrapped in a white piece of cloth. And the burning pyre in a corner of the compound.... From then on she was left in his care. They were always good friends. Even though they lived in a big city and she was sent to posh schools, he insisted that his daughter should learn Malayalam. They made it a rule that they would speak only in Malayalam at home. He used to say always that he cannot imagine about a girl who cannot sing soothing lullabies in the mother tongue.

While driving the car looking at the sunlit road, she felt that there was a thin layer over her eyes. It was thickening slowly. A cry of desperation began to surge up from the bottom of her heart. She slowed the car down to a halt at a turning where there was not much traffic, and started to sob gently, pressing her face against the steering.

He did not try to console her. Let her cry for some time, that might have a soothing effect on her, he thought.

When she raised her head, he noticed that her face was wet with tears.

After a while she fell into his lap with a loud cry. The same three year old girl who could not stand even the slightest pain.

"Calm down, baby, I can understand you now. Don't worry, we have been good friends all along and we will continue to be so." He patted her on the head.

Translation of Talamuṟakaḷ

✦ ✦ ✦

15

My Mother's Prayers

I have heard often that I was born out of my mother's continuous prayers. Nobody in our family had any doubt that all the late marriages and late pregnancies were the blessings of our family deity and that the departed souls of our ancestors, who float around in the sky have deep roots in our soil also.

But it was to which god or goddess had my mother prayed?

When I failed in the seventh standard examination for the first time I heard my mother wailing, invoking some unknown deity. As her cry and lamentations got mixed up, I could not understand why she cried. I did not ask her to whom she had complained, because the mothers of all the middle class families in our countryside had a number of gods and goddesses to choose from, to whom they could cry out all their grievances.

Anyway, I could not get through the seventh standard examination in my second attempt as well. Actually, it was not a tough examination. Even our maid servant's daughter could pass it without any difficulty. Hence my repeated failure in grappling with the examinations shocked my mother. While beating her breasts incessantly she looked at me with utter disbelief and her prayers thereafter turned out to be in the nature of some private complaints.

My mother never entered the puja room where our family deity and the departed souls of our ancestors were housed. There was a very narrow room on the southern corner of the passage between the bedrooms. My mother kept this dark, unventilated room as her own. At dawn and dusk she sat alone in it, keeping the door shut. Only once did I dare to enter that room. Then my mother caught me red-handed and pushed me out of the room. Thereafter I did not even look in the direction of that room.

I remember it was not like a normal prayer room. Pictures or idols of various gods, usually found in prayer rooms, were conspicuously absent in that room. The only thing I could see in it was a small pedestal. It might be on this pedestal that my mother sat cross-legged while praying, I thought.

My mother never visited temples. She was averse to fast and such other religious rituals. She had insisted that no funeral rites should be performed after her death. In the letter that she sent me after her second cardiac arrest she reminded me of this and had also put down several other conditions.

"As you know, all the mango trees in our homestead are of rare quality and the mere smell of the fruits itself is mouth-watering. They were all planted and nurtured by me and hence no mango tree should be felled for preparing my funeral pyre. You can get disks of dried cow dung from Arankavil Subran. Wrap my body neatly in a white piece of cloth, lay it on the pile of cow dung and burn it as quickly as possible without causing much pain. That is the one and only responsibility you have towards the dead. Don't perform the usual rituals of immersing the ashes and bones in a holy river, and the normal obsequies for fifteen days. The ashes and bones of all creatures are to become part of the soil. Ashes have a natural purity of their own and I don't want the polluted waters of the holy rivers to contaminate that purity...."

The conditions set forward by her were specific and well-reasoned.

"...Don't bother about offering rice-balls to my departed soul on the anniversaries of my death. Do you believe that I will come back in the form of a long-necked dirty crow to peck at your boiled rice and sesame seed, especially after having cut off all the links with this world? In fact, I hate the crows. Not just the hatred for the shining black colour; but the disgust for a creature that feeds on human excreta and garbage. How can I look on such a creature as a holy bird that comes to peck at the rice-ball meant for the departed souls...?"

As I was just a child then, I did not understand anything my mother said. Even my friends who came to my house occasionally had remarked that my mother's way of talking was quite strange; something like a tough fruit whose husk couldn't be broken easily so as to remove the seeds and devour the fruit inside.

Possibly because I was born out of her prolonged prayers that my mother had some special concern for me; and a little fear too. And that must be reason why she never beat me, whatever mischief I got into. When my deeds became unbearable to her, she would sit alone somewhere and cry for some time.

I never asked any questions to my mother, especially because she had a special skill in eluding questions. If at all she gave an answer that would be quite baffling.

Especially to the question about my father....

Whenever I asked her about my father, a smile would appear on her face.

Once she hinted that it was foolishness to ask about one's father.

"Why should a son know who his father is? What is the relevance of even the concept of fatherhood in his life?"

Later on, I felt it to be more or less true. 'Still, isn't it good to have a father to speak about and to show to others, just as the other children do?'

At first I tried to dismiss the thought, but it grew inside me and began to haunt me. Hence I was forced to seek an answer from my mother.

This time, however, she blushed scarlet and her lips quivered.

"Why do you want to know?"

I did not reply.

'Come on, tell me what do you want to know?"

"My father...."

"Who else, but that burly Raman Nair, the mahout? Are you satisfied now?"

When I noticed that my mother was shaking like a possessed woman, I ran away in great fear.

However, I knew very well that Raman Nair was not my father. In those days Kutttikrishnan, the elephant at the local chieftain's residence and its strong mahout Raman Nair were the two notables in our village. I had heard stories of the mothers of eligible village girls lamenting about their daughters not getting pregnant in time, although Raman Nair used to pass through their country by-lanes. Possibly, Raman Nair, capable of controlling the haughty Kuttikrishnan had emerged as one of the strongest father images in the village.

I was sure, however, that my mother, who hated the black crow, had nothing but hatred for the dark, round and bulky figure of Raman Nair; besides, his body was full of dark, curly tufts of hair.

Anyway, I realised then that as a father image Kochunni Thamburan and Raman Nair were similar.

Though I managed to get a pass in the seventh standard examination at last, I failed the Eighth standard examination repeatedly, and I think it was then that my mother realised the futility of her incessant prayers and the kind of lukewarm responses she had received from the gods above from time to time.

When she came back after meeting my class teacher Padmavathy madam, my mother told me:

"You will never be all right, Kunjoottan."

I looked at her questioningly.

"That is what Padmavathy teacher says."

When I stared at her as if asking whether she believed what the teacher had said, she mumbled:

"How can I disbelieve the words of those who have assumed the duty of teaching and enlightening children?"

Still my mother forgave me. However, when she came to know of my attempt to untie the skirt string of Sumavali, the youngest daughter of the charwoman, at a twilight behind the cowshed, my mother flew into a rage.

"It is true that you are the son of that wretched Raman Nair; there's no doubt about it. You have got the character of that bug-eyed buffalo."

While saying so my mother's voice quivered. It seemed that she was trying to push all the prayers and cries that she had uttered till then back into her heart.

After that she was seen lost in thought for some time. Then she said as if she had done some rethinking:

"Perhaps, what Padmavathy teacher said is true. I am quite sure now that you will never be all right, because I myself don't know to whom I have been praying so far."

I remember that while saying this, a kind of primitive calmness was settled down on her face. I stood perplexed for a long time without understanding the meaning of what she had said.

These are all old stories.

My mother died last week.

When I got the news, I asked my cousins over the phone that the funeral should be conducted only after my arrival from Ras-al-khaima in the Middle-east.

I was very much insistent that my mother's body should be cremated with all the rites and rituals. Hence the huge mango tree on the northern side of our compound was ordered to be felled to make the pyre. That was the normal custom followed in all the reputed families of our village.

The ceremony of collecting her bones and ashes from the cremation ground was held today. Now I am sitting in the train bound for Rameswaram, with a pot containing her bones and ashes, covered with red silk.

Those who are going to Rameswaram cannot but think about the departed souls. Among all those unpleasant memories, answer to a baffling question was still clouding my mind—to whom was my mother praying all these days?

Translation of Enṯe ammayuṭe prārthanakaḷ

✦ ✦ ✦

Sethu

A prominent modernist writer of Malayalam and a winner of the Sahitya Akademi and Kerala Sahitya Akademi awards, he has around thirty-five titles of novels and stories to his credit. Many of his works have been translated into other languages. Three of his stories have been filmed in Malayalam and one in Bengali.

A banker by profession, he is now the Chairman of the National Book Trust, India.

The Translator

Dr. Aboobacker Kappad, is a writer in Malayalam and translator. There are eight books in Malayalam to his credit, novels, short story collections, children's books and Cultural study. He retired as Associate Professor of English from Government College, Koyilandy (Kerala).

The Book

In this collection of fifteen distinctly different stories, the author delves deep into the human psyche observing the myriad intricacies of human behaviour, enticing the readers with the unexpected excitements and fulfilments of prophesies long made and revelations freshly deciphered. The line between the real and unreal is very thin and much more than observing the outer periphery of human existence, Sethu explores the wondrous world of archetypes, dreams, fantasies and nightmares, shedding precious light on the enigmas of existence.